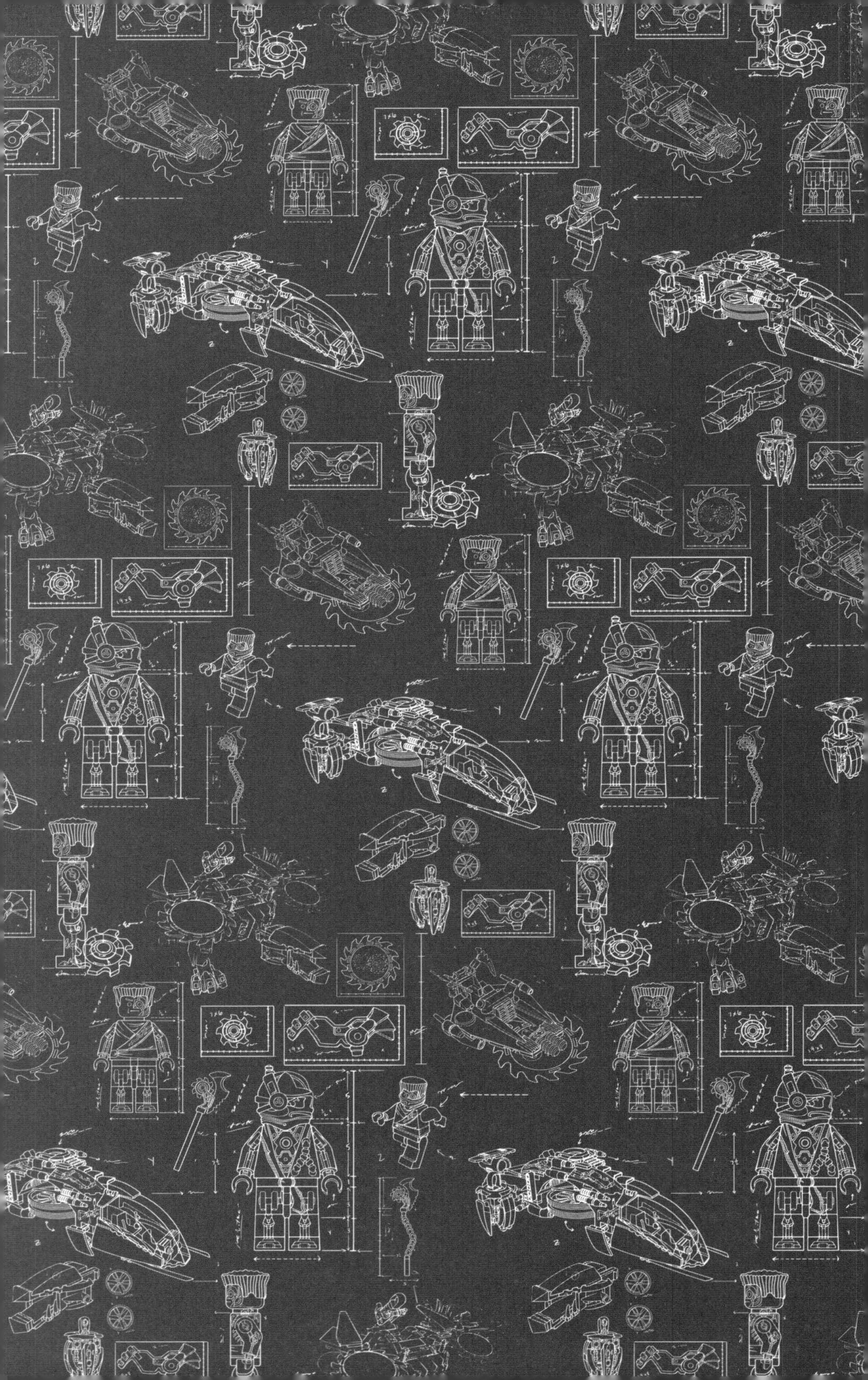

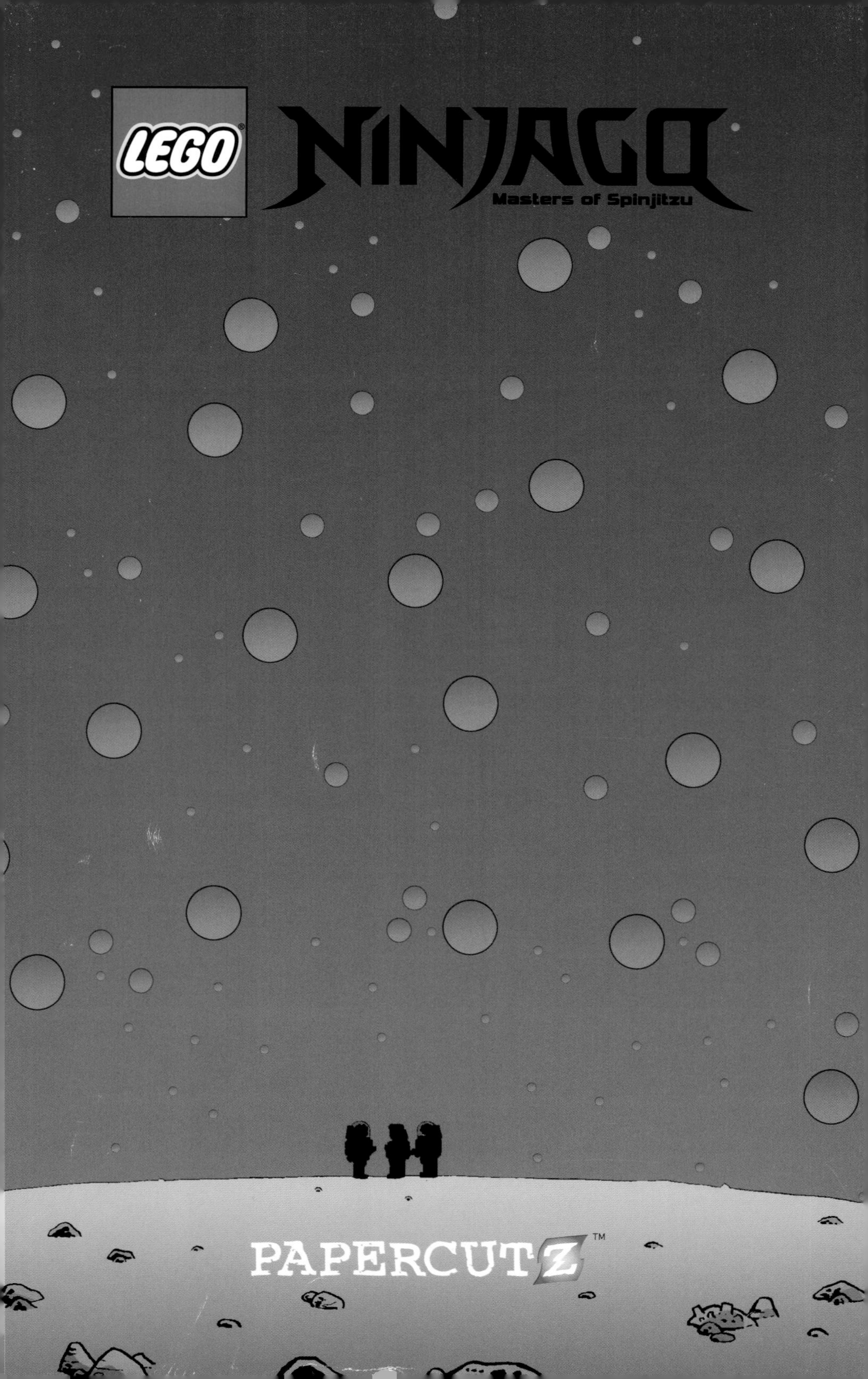
LEGO
NINJAGO
Masters of Spinjitzu
PAPERCUTZ™

LEGO® GRAPHIC NOVELS AVAILABLE FROM PAPERCUT

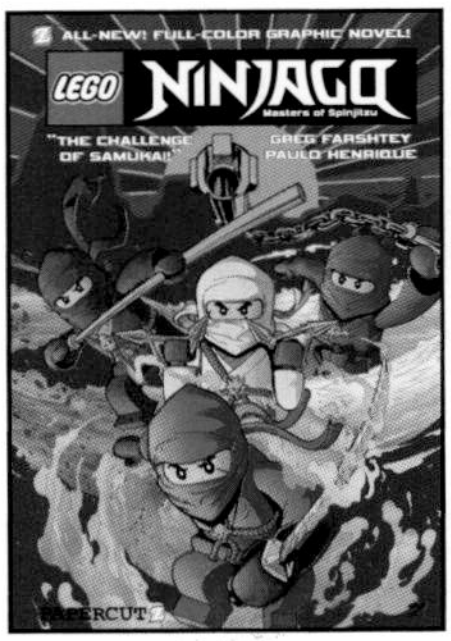

ALL-NEW! FULL-COLOR GRAPHIC NOVEL!
LEGO NINJAGO
"THE CHALLENGE OF SAMUKAI!"
GREG FARSHTEY
PAULO HENRIQUE
PAPERCUT

LEGO NINJAGO #1

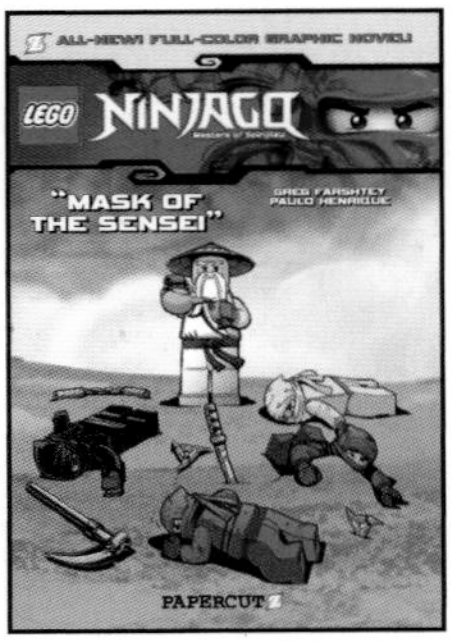

ALL-NEW! FULL-COLOR GRAPHIC NOVEL!
LEGO NINJAGO
"MASK OF THE SENSEI"
GREG FARSHTEY
PAULO HENRIQUE
PAPERCUT

LEGO NINJAGO #2

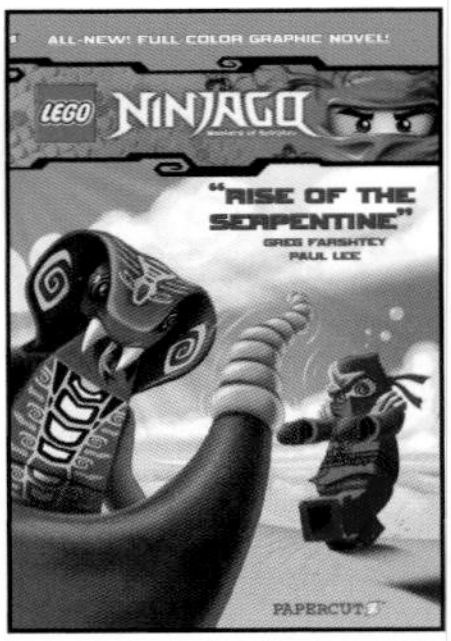

ALL-NEW! FULL COLOR GRAPHIC NOVEL!
LEGO NINJAGO
"RISE OF THE SERPENTINE"
GREG FARSHTEY
PAUL LEE
PAPERCUT

LEGO NINJAGO #3

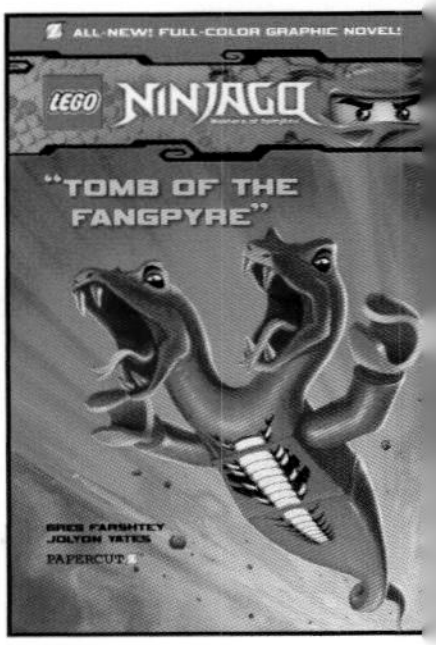

ALL-NEW! FULL-COLOR GRAPHIC NOVEL!
LEGO NINJAGO
"TOMB OF THE FANGPYRE"
GREG FARSHTEY
JOLYON YATES
PAPERCUT

LEGO NINJAGO #4

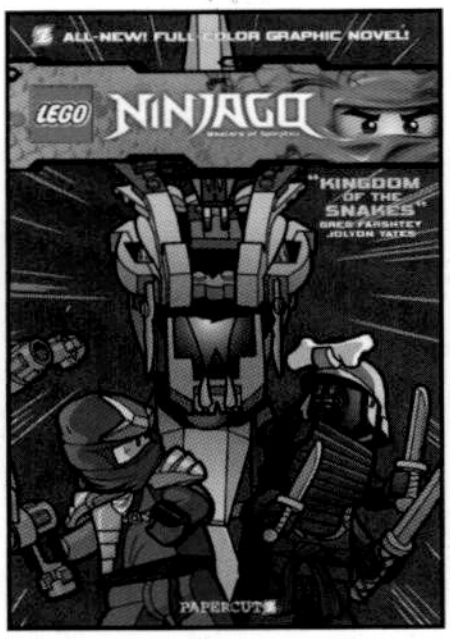

ALL-NEW! FULL-COLOR GRAPHIC NOVEL!
LEGO NINJAGO
"KINGDOM OF THE SNAKES"
GREG FARSHTEY
JOLYON YATES
PAPERCUT

LEGO NINJAGO #5

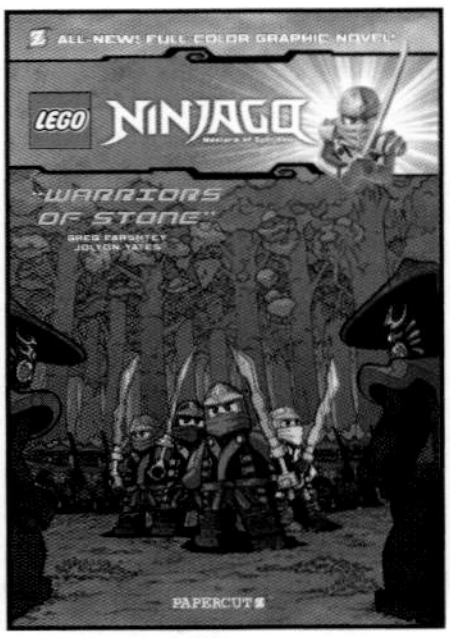

ALL-NEW! FULL COLOR GRAPHIC NOVEL!
LEGO NINJAGO
"WARRIORS OF STONE"
GREG FARSHTEY
JOLYON YATES
PAPERCUT

LEGO NINJAGO #6

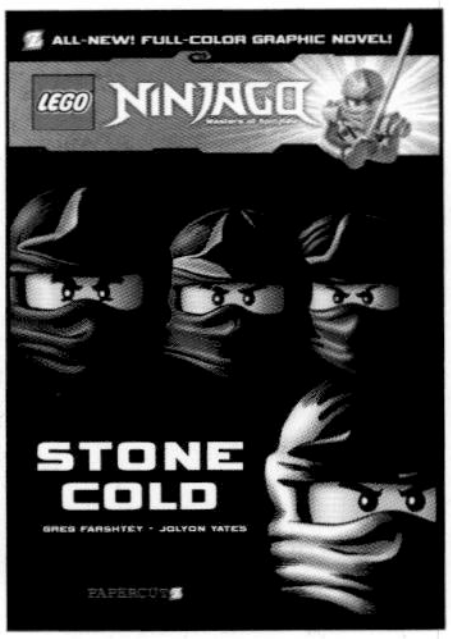

ALL-NEW! FULL-COLOR GRAPHIC NOVEL!
LEGO NINJAGO
STONE COLD
GREG FARSHTEY · JOLYON YATES
PAPERCUT

LEGO NINJAGO #7

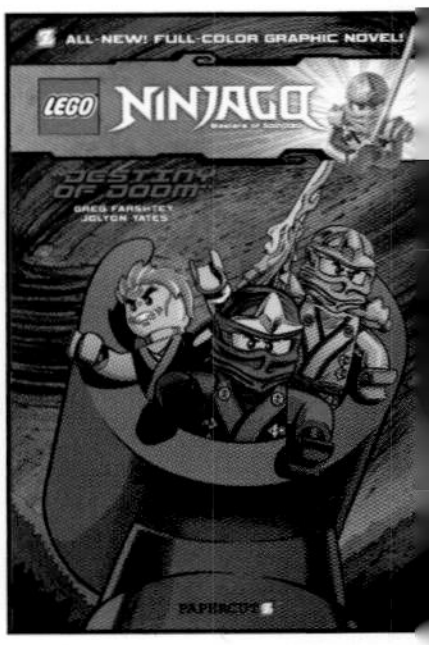

ALL-NEW! FULL-COLOR GRAPHIC NOVEL!
LEGO NINJAGO
DESTINY OF DOOM
GREG FARSHTEY
JOLYON YATES
PAPERCUT

LEGO NINJAGO #8

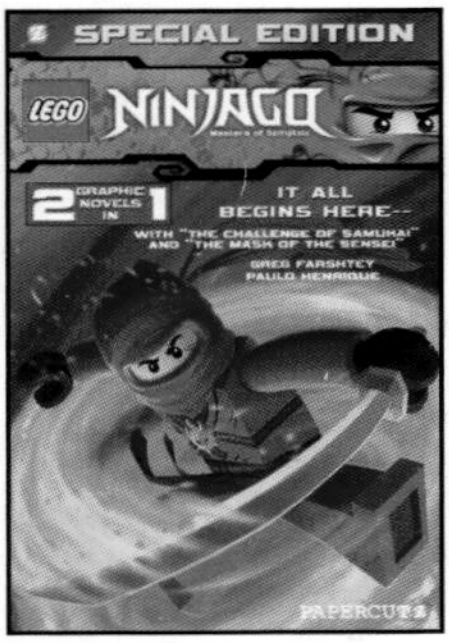

SPECIAL EDITION
LEGO NINJAGO
2 GRAPHIC NOVELS IN 1
IT ALL BEGINS HERE--
WITH "THE CHALLENGE OF SAMUKAI" AND "THE MASK OF THE SENSEI"
GREG FARSHTEY
PAULO HENRIQUE
PAPERCUT

SPECIAL EDITION #1
(Features stories from NINJAGO #1 & #2.)

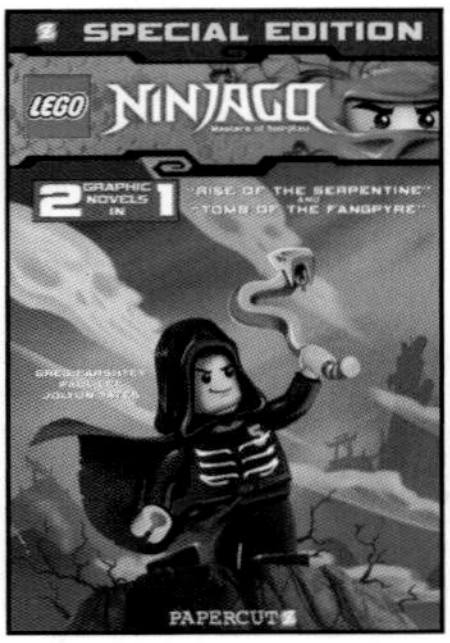

SPECIAL EDITION
LEGO NINJAGO
2 GRAPHIC NOVELS IN 1
"RISE OF THE SERPENTINE" AND "TOMB OF THE FANGPYRE"
GREG FARSHTEY
PAUL LEE
JOLYON YATES
PAPERCUT

SPECIAL EDITION #2
(Features stories from NINJAGO #3 & #4.)

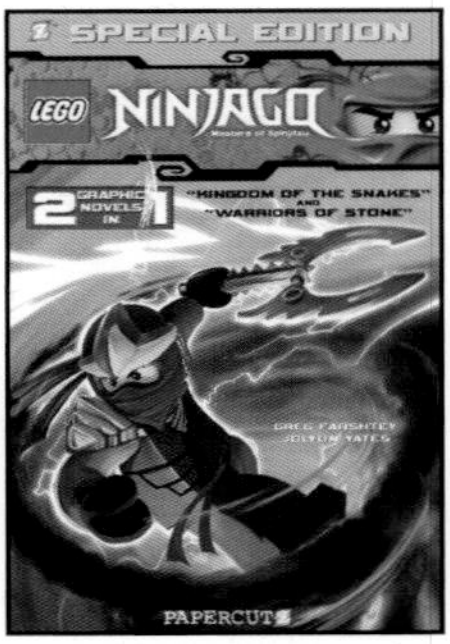

SPECIAL EDITION
LEGO NINJAGO
2 GRAPHIC NOVELS IN 1
"KINGDOM OF THE SNAKES" AND "WARRIORS OF STONE"
GREG FARSHTEY
JOLYON YATES
PAPERCUT

SPECIAL EDITION #3
(Features stories from NINJAGO #5 & #6.)

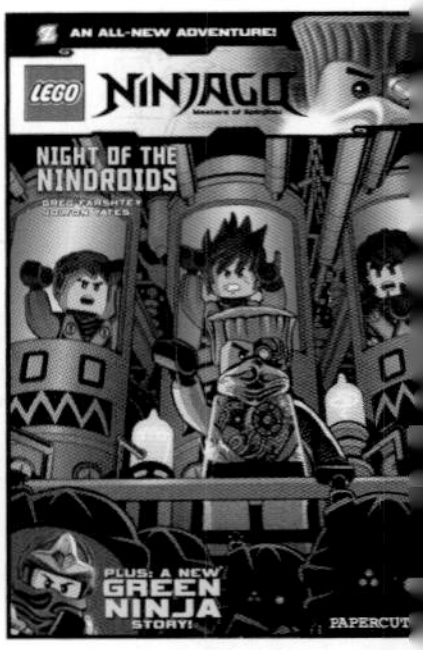

AN ALL-NEW ADVENTURE!
LEGO NINJAGO
NIGHT OF THE NINDROIDS
GREG FARSHTEY
JOLYON YATES
PLUS: A NEW GREEN NINJA STORY!
PAPERCUT

LEGO NINJAGO #9

LEGO® NINJAGO graphic novels are available in paperback and hardcover at booksellers everywhere.

LEGO® NINJAGO #1-10 are $6.99 in paperback, and $10.99 in hardcover. LEGO NINJAGO SPECIAL EDITION #1-3 are $10.99 in paperback only. You can also order online at papercutz.com. Or call 1-800-886-1223, Monday through Friday, 9 – 5 EST. MC, Visa, and AmEx accepted. To order by mail, please add $4.00 for postage and handling for first book ordered, $1.00 for each additional book and make check payable to NBM Publishing. Send to: Papercutz, 160 Broadway, Suite 700, East Wing, New York, NY 10038.

LEGO NINJAGO graphic novels are also available digitally wherever e-books are sold.

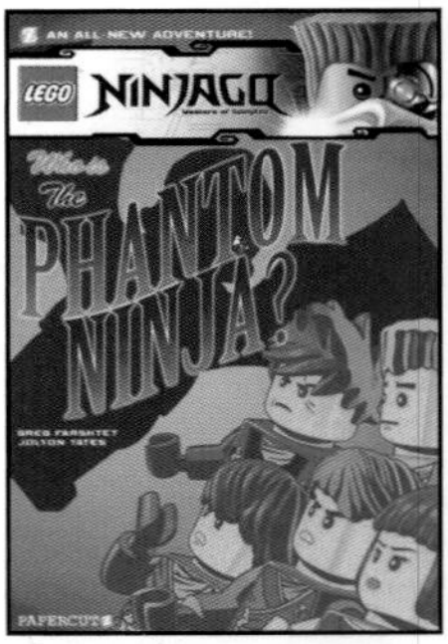

AN ALL-NEW ADVENTURE!
LEGO NINJAGO
Who is The PHANTOM NINJA?
GREG FARSHTEY
JOLYON YATES
PAPERCUT

LEGO NINJAGO #10

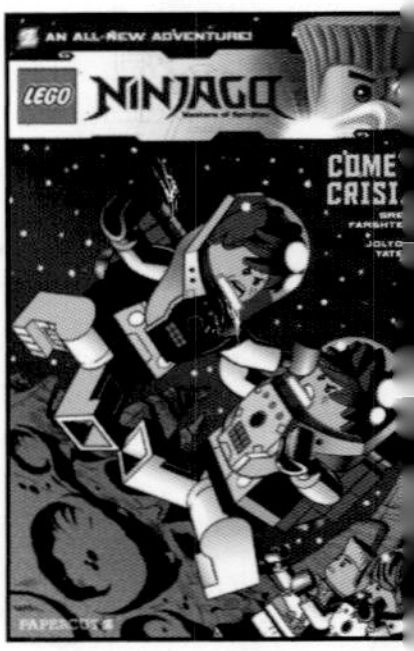

AN ALL-NEW ADVENTURE!
LEGO NINJAGO
COME
CRISI
PAPERCUT

LEGO NINJAGO #11

LEGO NINJAGO
Masters of Spinjitzu

"COMET CRISIS"

Greg Farshtey – Writer
Jolyon Yates – Artist
Laurie E. Smith – Colorist

PAPERCUTZ™
New York

LEGO® NINJAGO Masters of Spinjitzu
#11 "Comet Crisis"
Greg Farshtey – Writer
Jolyon Yates – Artist
Laurie E. Smith – Colorist
Bryan Senka – Letterer
Dawn K. Guzzo – Production
Beth Scorzato – Production Coordinator
Michael Petranek – Associate Editor

Jim Salicrup
Editor-in-Chief

ISBN: 978-1-62991-046-8 paperback edition
ISBN: 978-1-62991-047-5 hardcover edition

Papercutz books may be purchased for business or promotional use. For information on bulk pur-
chases please contact Macmillan Corporate and Premium Sales Department at (800) 221-7945 x5442

Printed in Canada
August 2014 by Friesens
1 Printers Way
Altona, MB R0G 0B0

Distributed by Macmillan
First Printing

FSC
www.fsc.org
MIX
Paper from
responsible sources
FSC® C016245

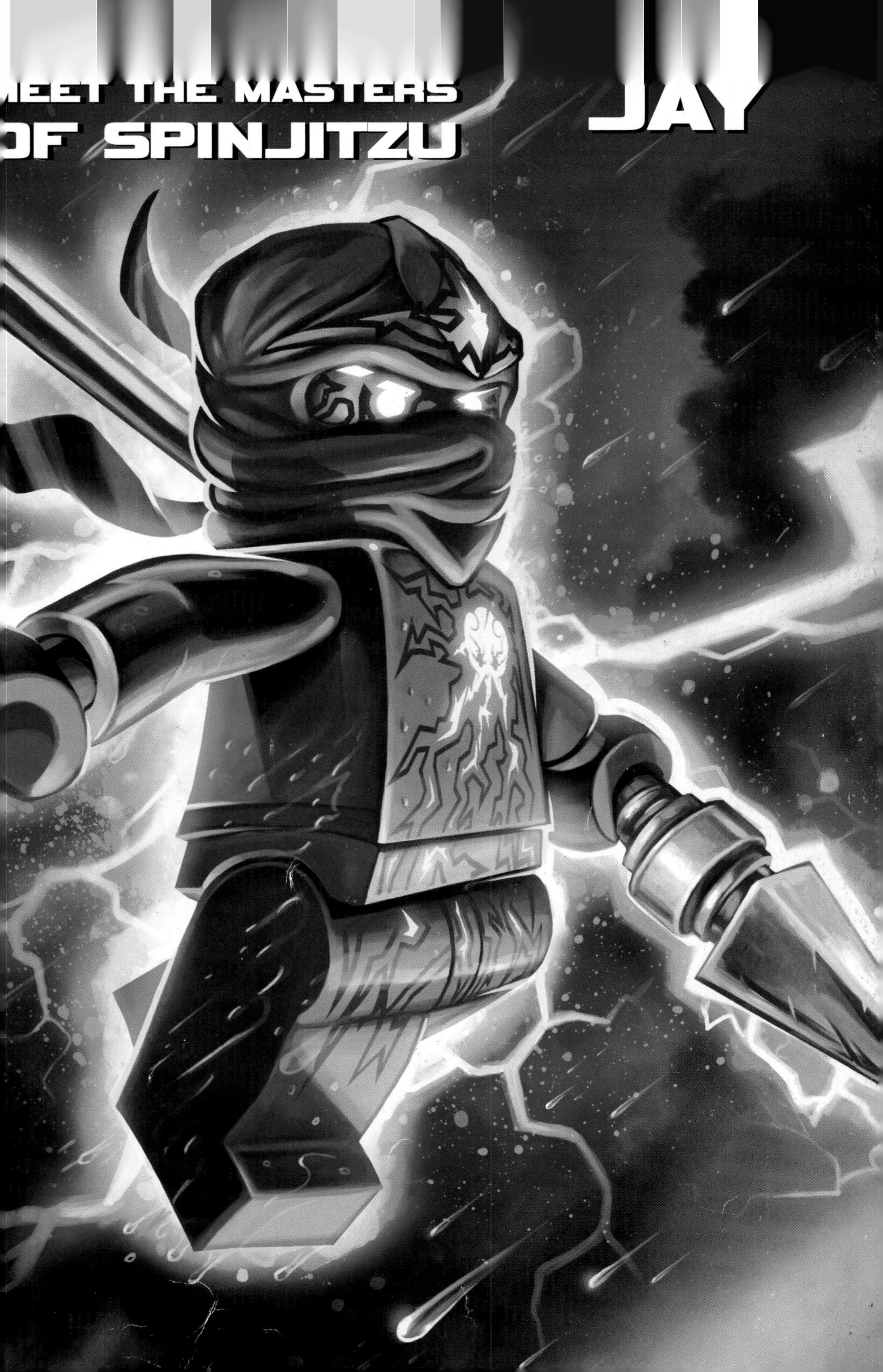
MEET THE MASTERS
OF SPINJITZU
JAY

COLE

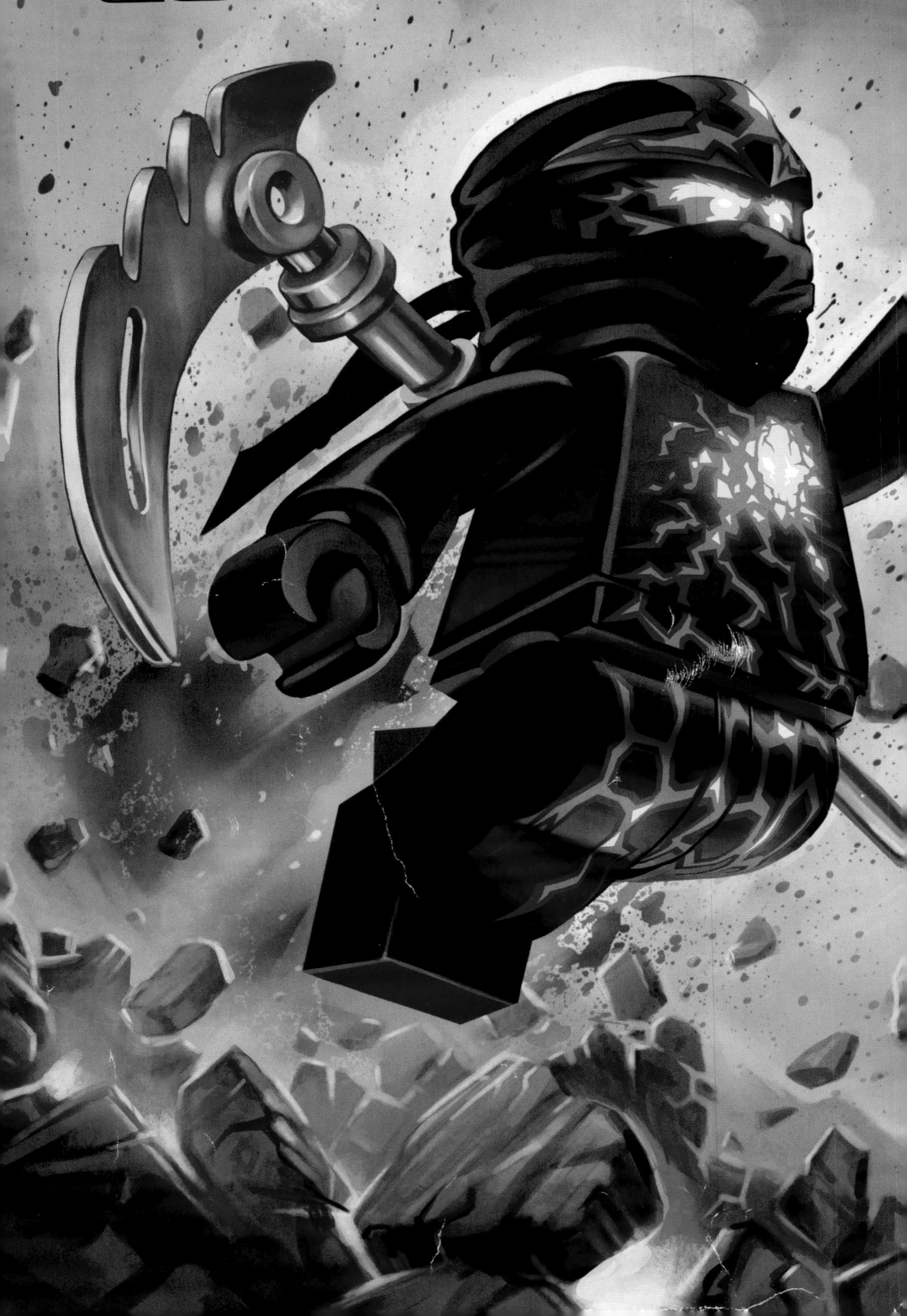

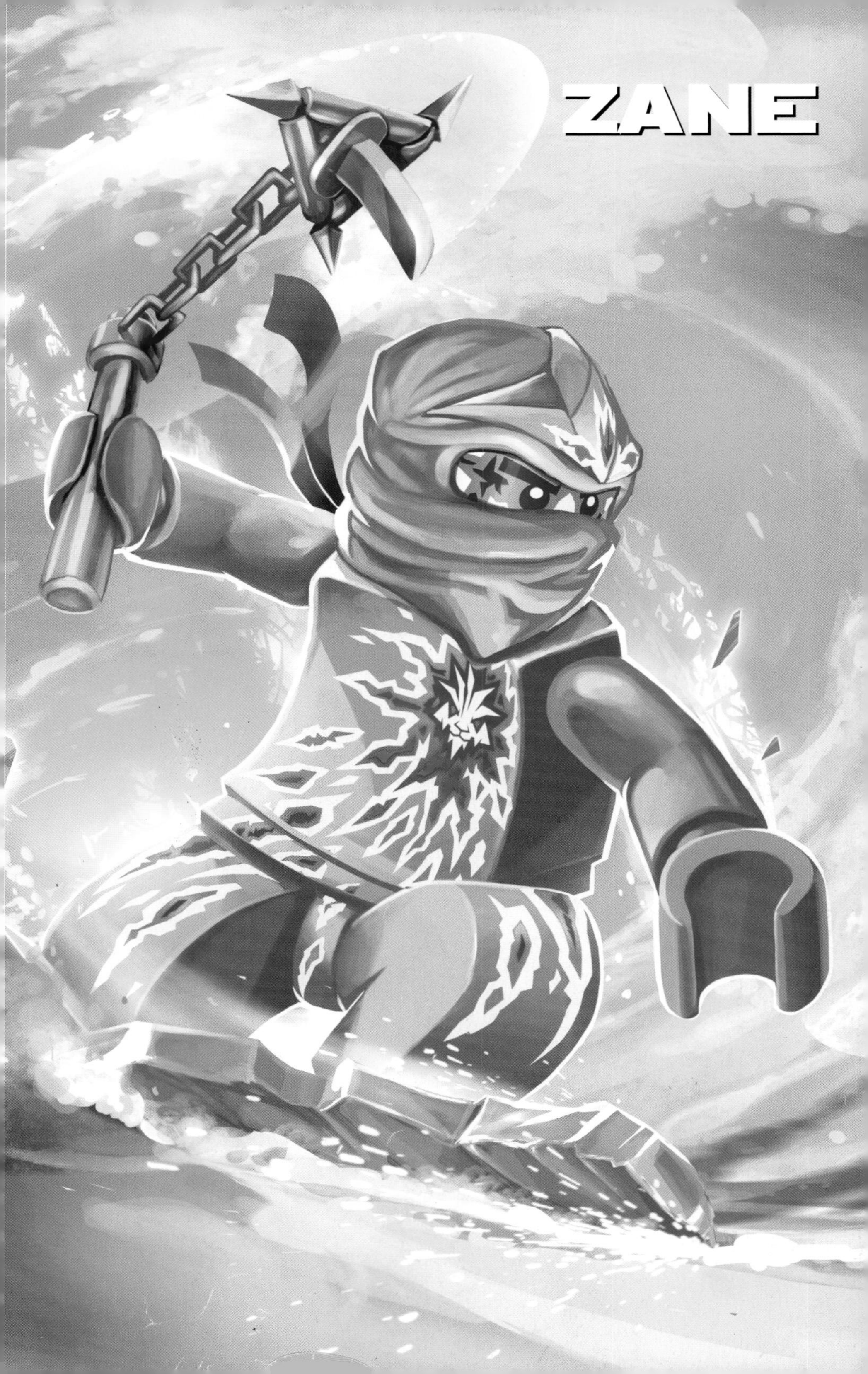
ZANE

KAI

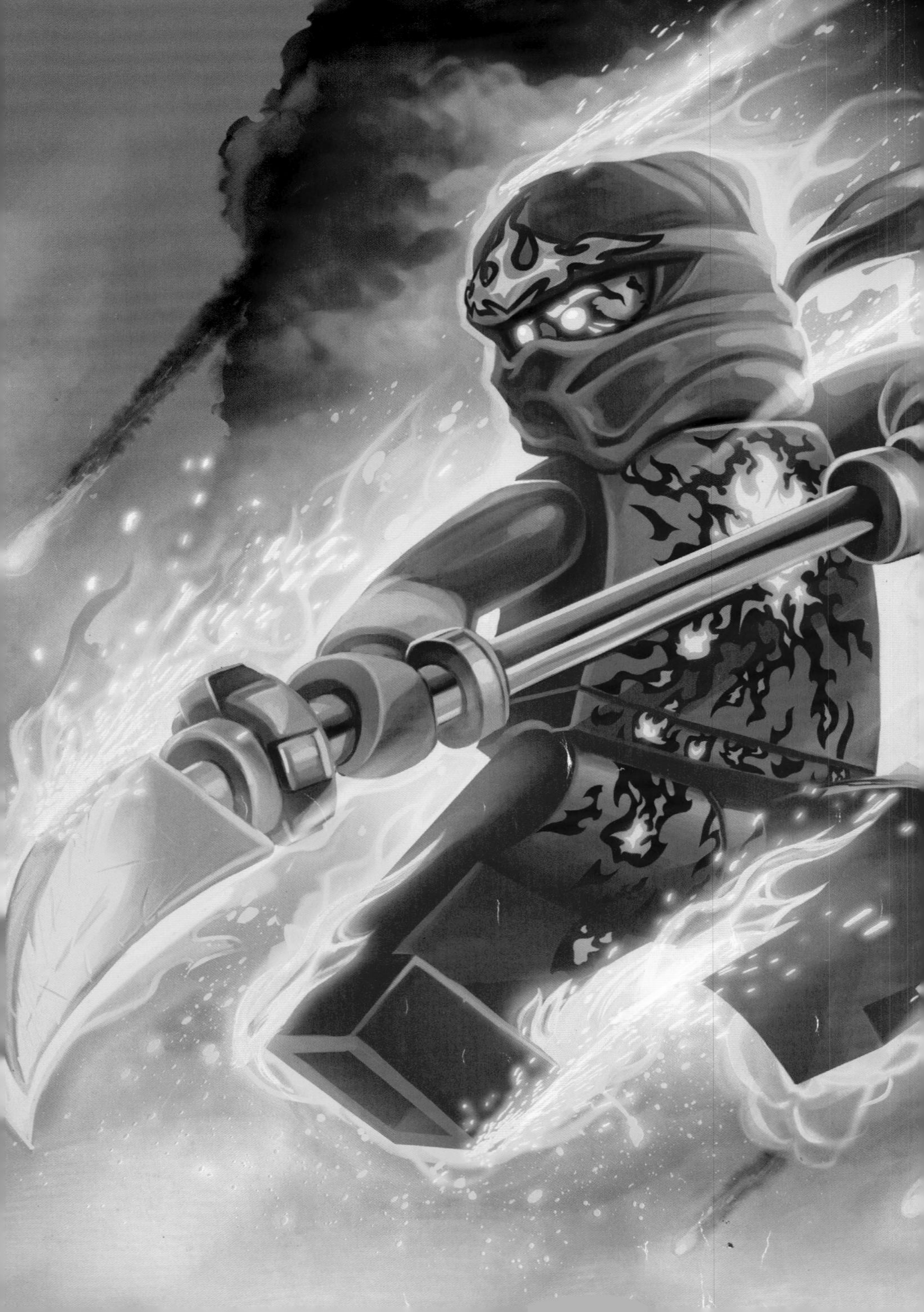

THOUSANDS OF ASTEROIDS PASS NINJAGO EVERY YEAR, AND NO ONE GIVES THEM A SECOND THOUGHT.

AFTER ALL, THEY'RE JUST HUNKS OF SPACE ROCK, RIGHT?

T WAS WHAT WE NINJA THOUGHT WHEN WE OWED AWAY ON **GENERAL CRYPTOR'S** SHIP AND WOUND UP ON WHAT WE AT FIRST HOUGHT WAS A COMET, BUT TURNED OUT TO BE SOMETHING VERY DIFFERENT."

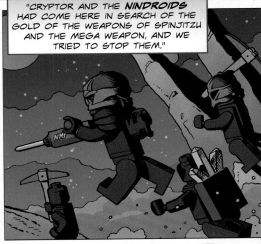

"CRYPTOR AND THE **NINDROIDS** HAD COME HERE IN SEARCH OF THE GOLD OF THE WEAPONS OF SPINJITZU AND THE MEGA WEAPON, AND WE TRIED TO STOP THEM."

WE FAILED. CRYPTOR AND THE NDROIDS ESCAPED, LEAVING US ANDED WITH A BROKEN STARSHIP."

WE WERE APPED AND NE... OR SO E THOUGHT."

WE HAD FORGOTTEN ONE THING:

AN ASTEROID TRAVELS THROUGH SPACE, AND ANYTHING THAT TRAVELS CAN CARRY...

A PASSEN-GER.

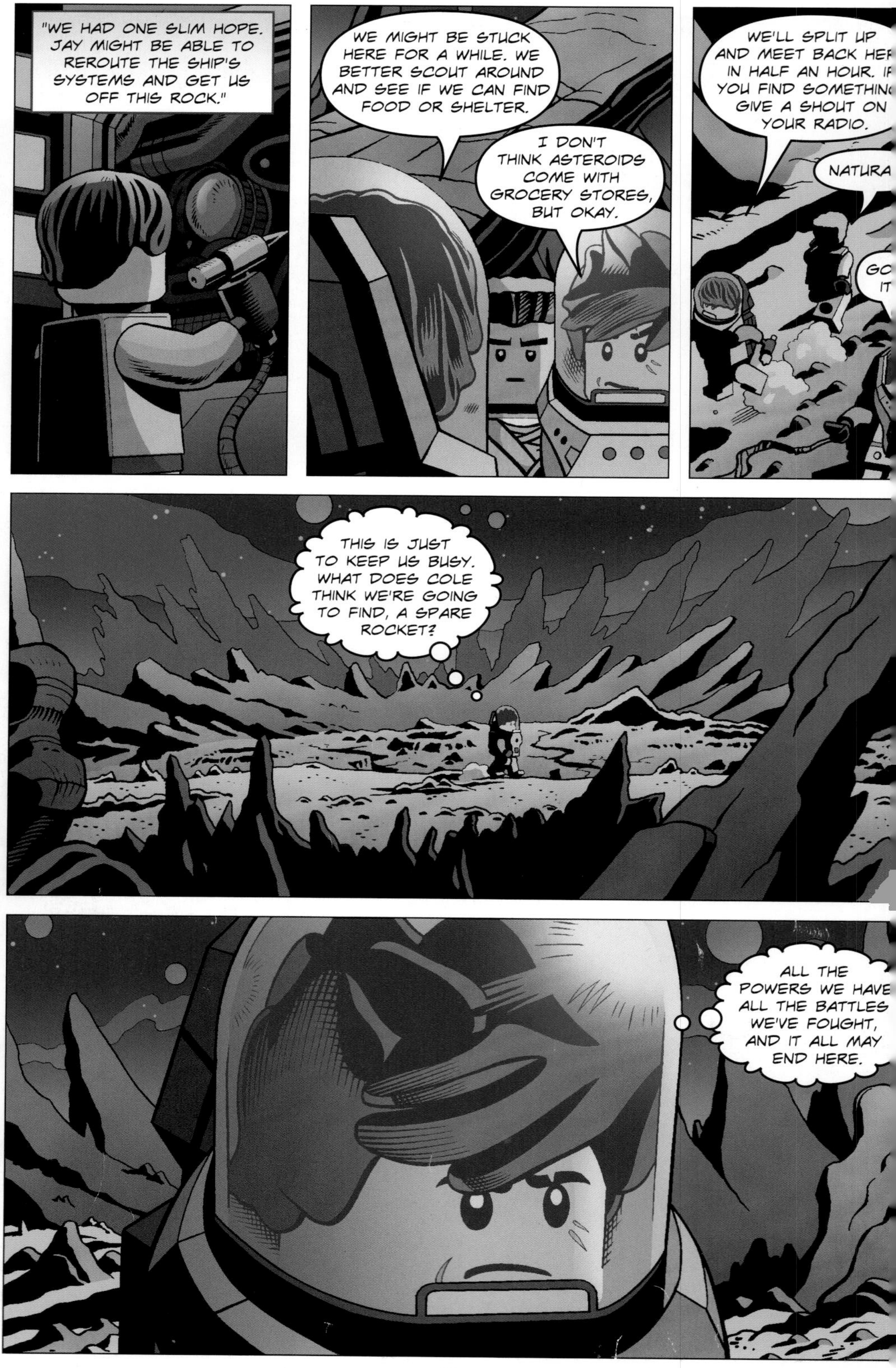
"WE HAD ONE SLIM HOPE. JAY MIGHT BE ABLE TO REROUTE THE SHIP'S SYSTEMS AND GET US OFF THIS ROCK."
WE MIGHT BE STUCK HERE FOR A WHILE. WE BETTER SCOUT AROUND AND SEE IF WE CAN FIND FOOD OR SHELTER.
I DON'T THINK ASTEROIDS COME WITH GROCERY STORES, BUT OKAY.
WE'LL SPLIT UP AND MEET BACK HER IN HALF AN HOUR. IF YOU FIND SOMETHIN GIVE A SHOUT ON YOUR RADIO.
NATURA
THIS IS JUST TO KEEP US BUSY. WHAT DOES COLE THINK WE'RE GOING TO FIND, A SPARE ROCKET?
ALL THE POWERS WE HAVE ALL THE BATTLES WE'VE FOUGHT, AND IT ALL MAY END HERE.

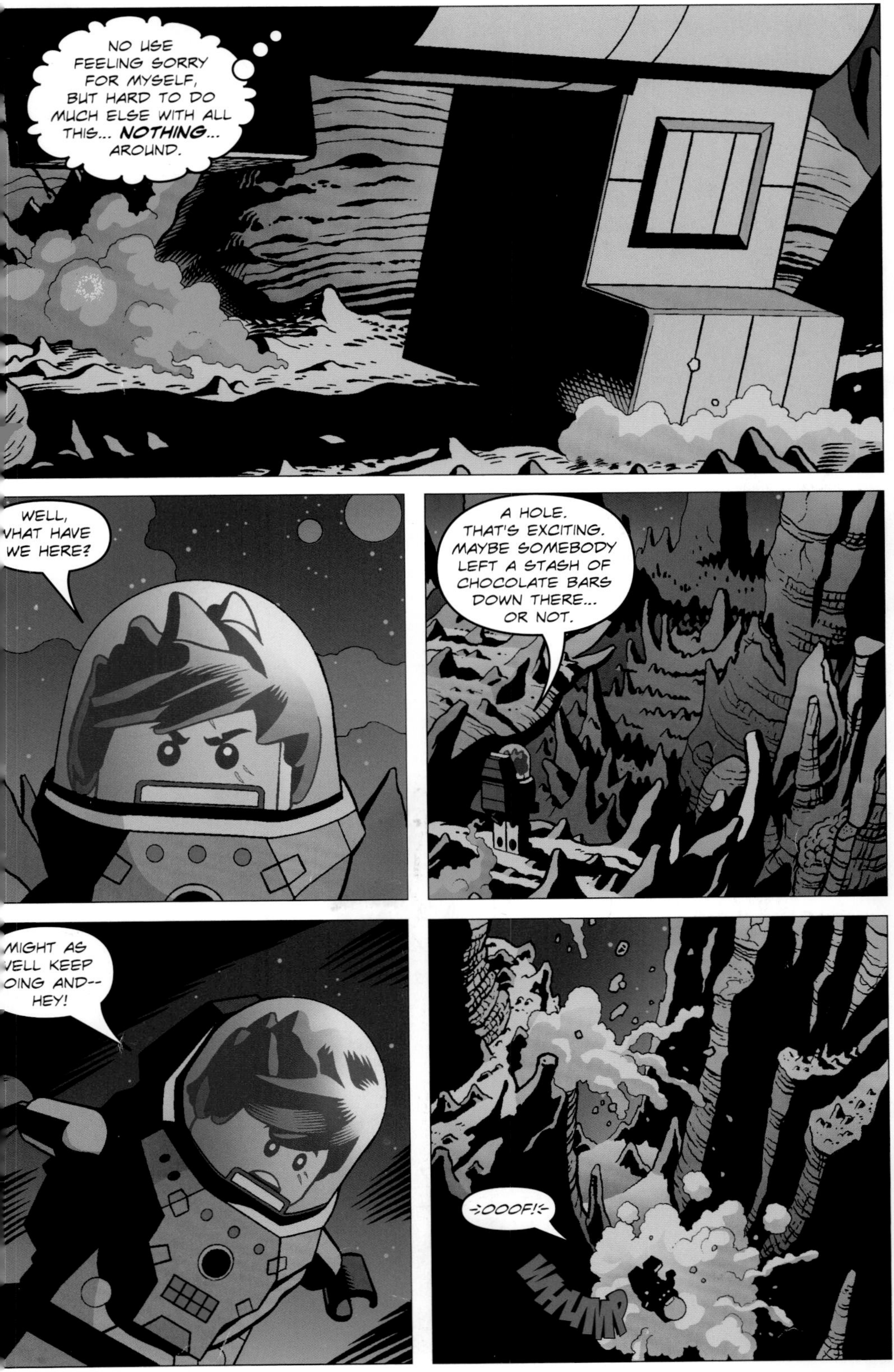
NO USE FEELING SORRY FOR MYSELF, BUT HARD TO DO MUCH ELSE WITH ALL THIS... NOTHING... AROUND.
WELL, WHAT HAVE WE HERE?
A HOLE. THAT'S EXCITING. MAYBE SOMEBODY LEFT A STASH OF CHOCOLATE BARS DOWN THERE... OR NOT.
MIGHT AS WELL KEEP OING AND-- HEY!
OOOF!
WHUMP

THAT'S FUNNY. FOR A SECOND, I THOUGHT I SAW... NAH, COULDN'T BE.

FACE IT, NINJA-- YOU COULD BE STUCK HERE A LONG TIME.

AND WHEN WE R OUT OF FOO CAPSULES A WATER...

THIS IS ALL MY FAULT! I SHOULD HAVE BEEN MORE AWARE.

I SHOULD HAVE REALIZED THE **OVERLORD** MIGHT FIND A WAY TO COME BACK.

BUT, NO. WE THOUGHT OUR BATTLES WERE WON.

WE BECAME TEACHERS. WE GOT COMFORTABLE AND LAZY, AND NOW IT'S TOO LATE.

IT'S NEVER TOO LATE, COLE.

HUH?

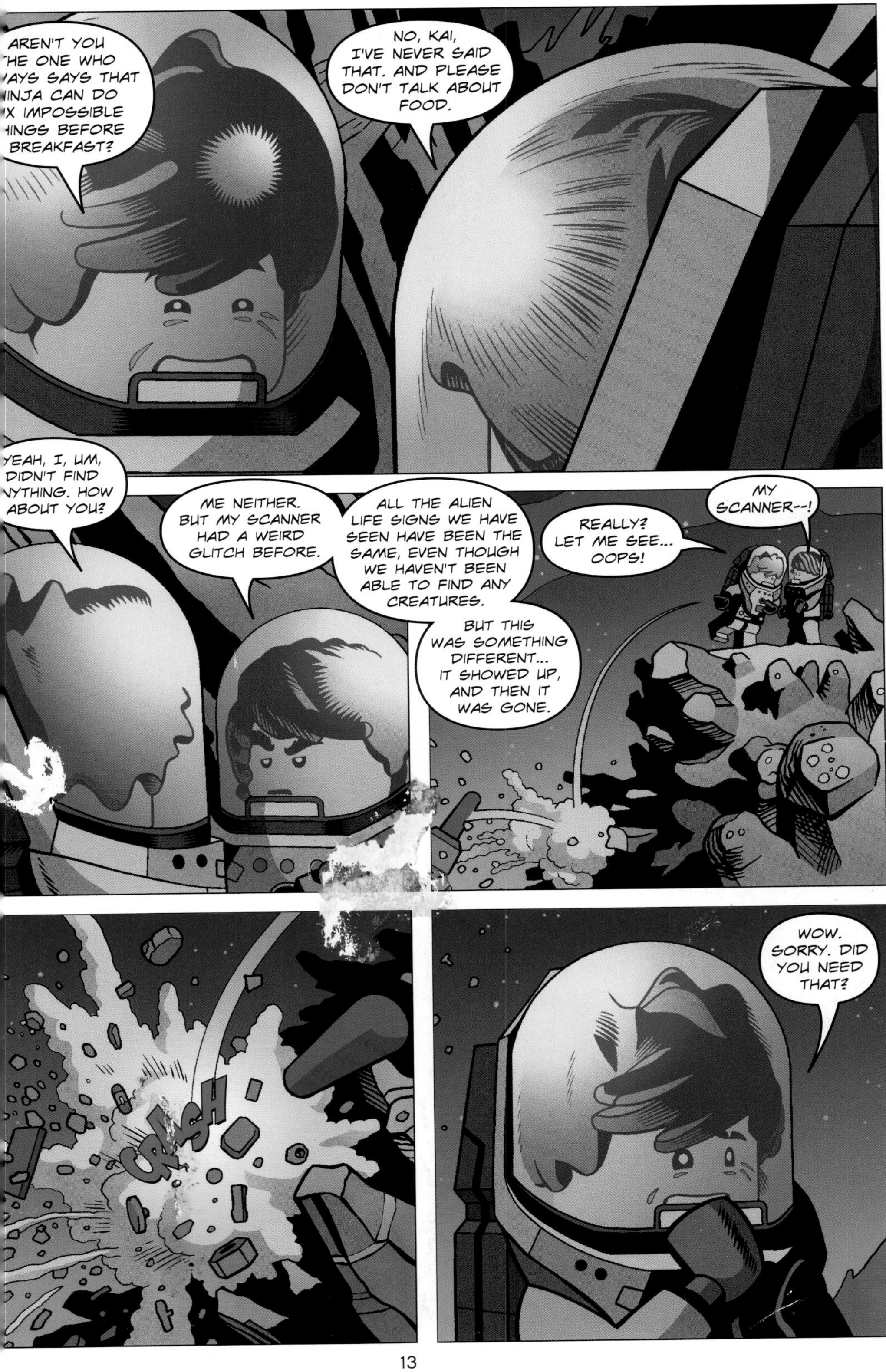

AREN'T YOU HE ONE WHO AYS SAYS THAT INJA CAN DO X IMPOSSIBLE HINGS BEFORE BREAKFAST?
NO, KAI, I'VE NEVER SAID THAT. AND PLEASE DON'T TALK ABOUT FOOD.
YEAH, I, UM, DIDN'T FIND NYTHING. HOW ABOUT YOU?
ME NEITHER. BUT MY SCANNER HAD A WEIRD GLITCH BEFORE.
ALL THE ALIEN LIFE SIGNS WE HAVE SEEN HAVE BEEN THE SAME, EVEN THOUGH WE HAVEN'T BEEN ABLE TO FIND ANY CREATURES.
BUT THIS WAS SOMETHING DIFFERENT... IT SHOWED UP, AND THEN IT WAS GONE.
REALLY? LET ME SEE... OOPS!
MY SCANNER--!
CRASH
WOW. SORRY. DID YOU NEED THAT?

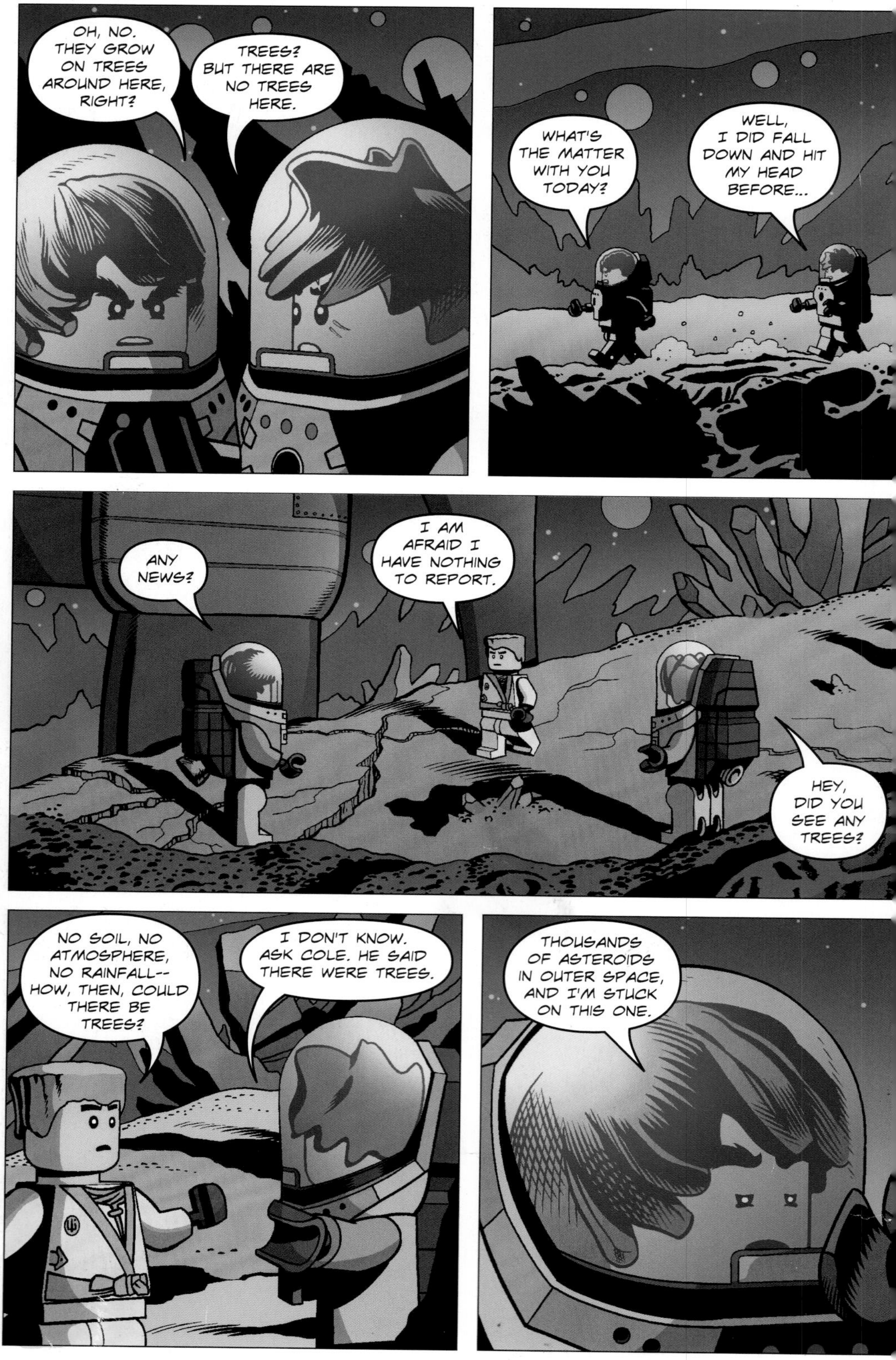
OH, NO. THEY GROW ON TREES AROUND HERE, RIGHT?
TREES? BUT THERE ARE NO TREES HERE.
WHAT'S THE MATTER WITH YOU TODAY?
WELL, I DID FALL DOWN AND HIT MY HEAD BEFORE...
ANY NEWS?
I AM AFRAID I HAVE NOTHING TO REPORT.
HEY, DID YOU SEE ANY TREES?
NO SOIL, NO ATMOSPHERE, NO RAINFALL-- HOW, THEN, COULD THERE BE TREES?
I DON'T KNOW. ASK COLE. HE SAID THERE WERE TREES.
THOUSANDS OF ASTEROIDS IN OUTER SPACE, AND I'M STUCK ON THIS ONE.

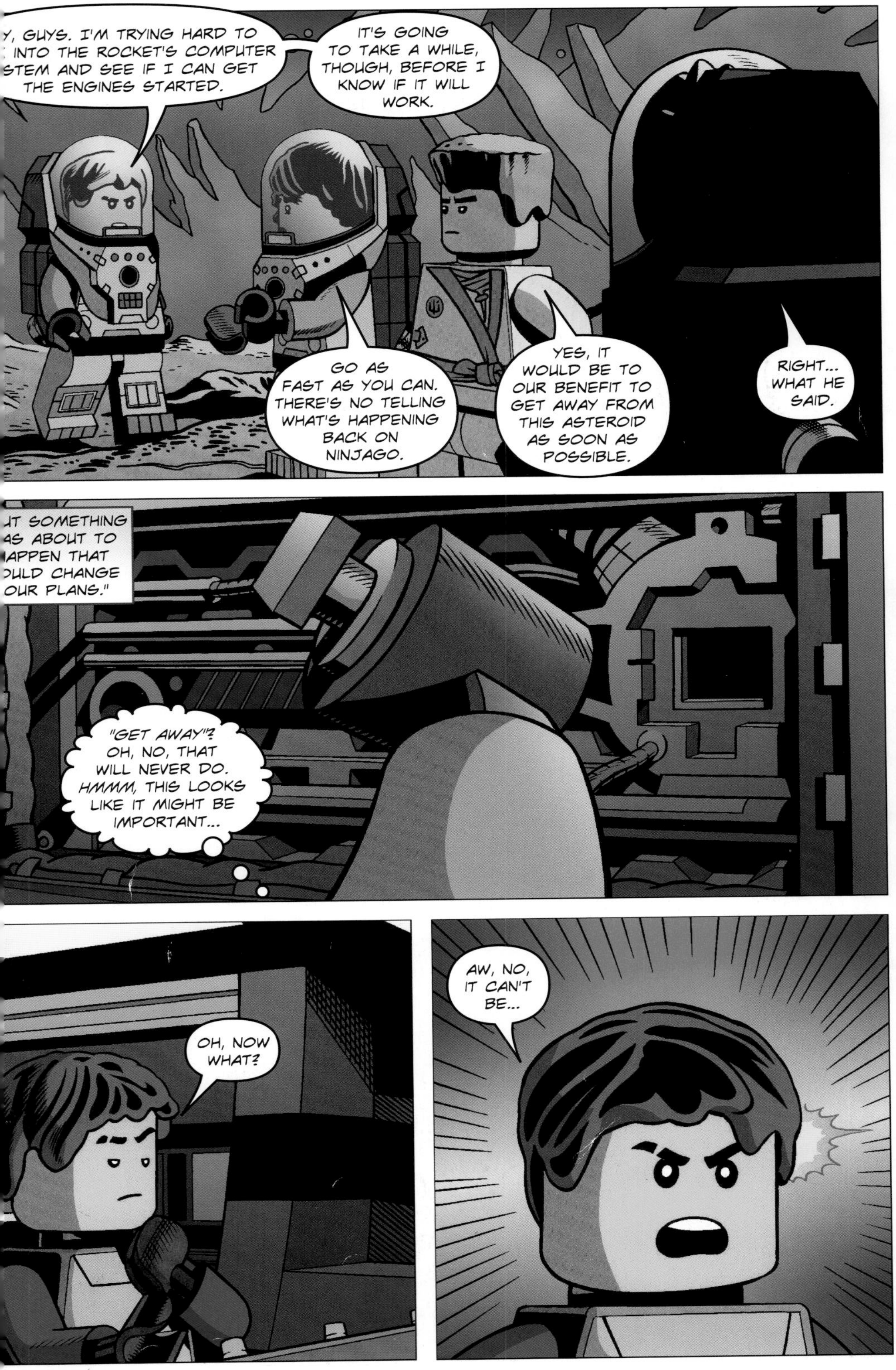
Y, GUYS. I'M TRYING HARD TO INTO THE ROCKET'S COMPUTER STEM AND SEE IF I CAN GET THE ENGINES STARTED.
IT'S GOING TO TAKE A WHILE, THOUGH, BEFORE I KNOW IF IT WILL WORK.
GO AS FAST AS YOU CAN. THERE'S NO TELLING WHAT'S HAPPENING BACK ON NINJAGO.
YES, IT WOULD BE TO OUR BENEFIT TO GET AWAY FROM THIS ASTEROID AS SOON AS POSSIBLE.
RIGHT... WHAT HE SAID.
UT SOMETHING AS ABOUT TO APPEN THAT OULD CHANGE OUR PLANS."
"GET AWAY"? OH, NO, THAT WILL NEVER DO. HMMM, THIS LOOKS LIKE IT MIGHT BE IMPORTANT...
OH, NOW WHAT?
AW, NO, IT CAN'T BE...

IT'S GONE! IT'S GONE!

SLOW DOWN, WHAT'S GONE?

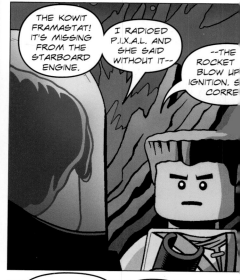

THE KOWIT FRAMASTAT! IT'S MISSING FROM THE STARBOARD ENGINE.

I RADIOED P.I.X.A.L. AND SHE SAID WITHOUT IT--

--THE ROCKET BLOW UP IGNITION. S CORRE

THEN WE BETTER FIND IT FAST, OR-- →OOF!←

HEY, WATCH WHERE YOU'RE GOING, KAI!

SORRY.

THAT MUST HAVE BEEN SOME BUMP ON THE HEAD.

ALL RIGHT, PARTNERS, LET'S START SEARCHING...

WITHOUT RUNNING EACH OTHER OVER, IF POSSIBLE.

THEY WILL NEVER STOP SEARCHING. I GUESS IT'S A GOOD THING I FOUND A CONVENIENT PLACE TO HIDE IT.

NO SIGN.

MAYBE WE'RE NOT LOOKING IN THE RIGHT PLACES...

I BELIEVE KAI HAS A POINT THOUGH MAYBE N THE ONE HE WAS INTENDING.

I DO NOT BELIEVE THE LIFE THAT EXISTS ON THIS ASTEROID CAPABLE OF THIS LEVEL OF SABOTAGE.

THE ONLY REASONABLE THEORY IS THAT ONE OF US TOOK THE PIECE.

SO WHAT, KAI, IS WHAT I SUPPOSE TO FIND OUT.

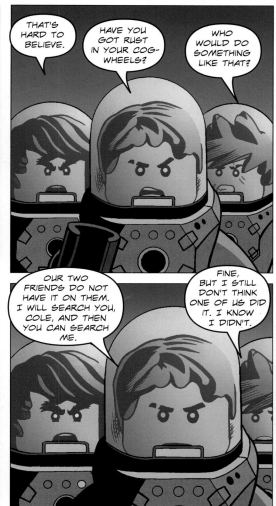

THAT'S HARD TO BELIEVE.

HAVE YOU GOT RUST IN YOUR COG-WHEELS?

WHO WOULD DO SOMETHING LIKE THAT?

OUR TWO FRIENDS DO NOT HAVE IT ON THEM. I WILL SEARCH YOU, COLE, AND THEN YOU CAN SEARCH ME.

FINE, BUT I STILL DON'T THINK ONE OF US DID IT. I KNOW I DIDN'T.

BUT, FINE, GO AHEAD AND-- HUH?

INDEED.

THAT'S IT. THAT'S THE FRAMASTAT.

PLEASE EXPLAIN. WHAT DID YOU HOPE TO GAIN BY SABOTAGING THE ROCKET?

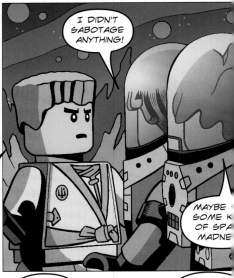

I DIDN'T SABOTAGE ANYTHING!

MAYBE SOME K OF SPA MADNE

COLE WOULDN'T DO THIS... WOULD YOU?

OR IS THE DIGITAL OVERLORD CONTROLLING YOU?

IF HE IS, COUGH OR SOMETHING SO WE'LL KNOW.

MAYBE YOU SHOULDN'T PUT THAT FRAMASTAT BACK IN.

WHAT IF HE TINKERE WITH IT? YO SHOULD TAK YOUR TIME A EXAMINE IT

TAK A LO TIM

YOU'RE ALL NUTS! SOMEONE STOLE THAT GIZMO, ALL RIGHT, AND THEN PLANTED IT ON ME.

AND I'M GOING TO FIND OUT **WHO!**

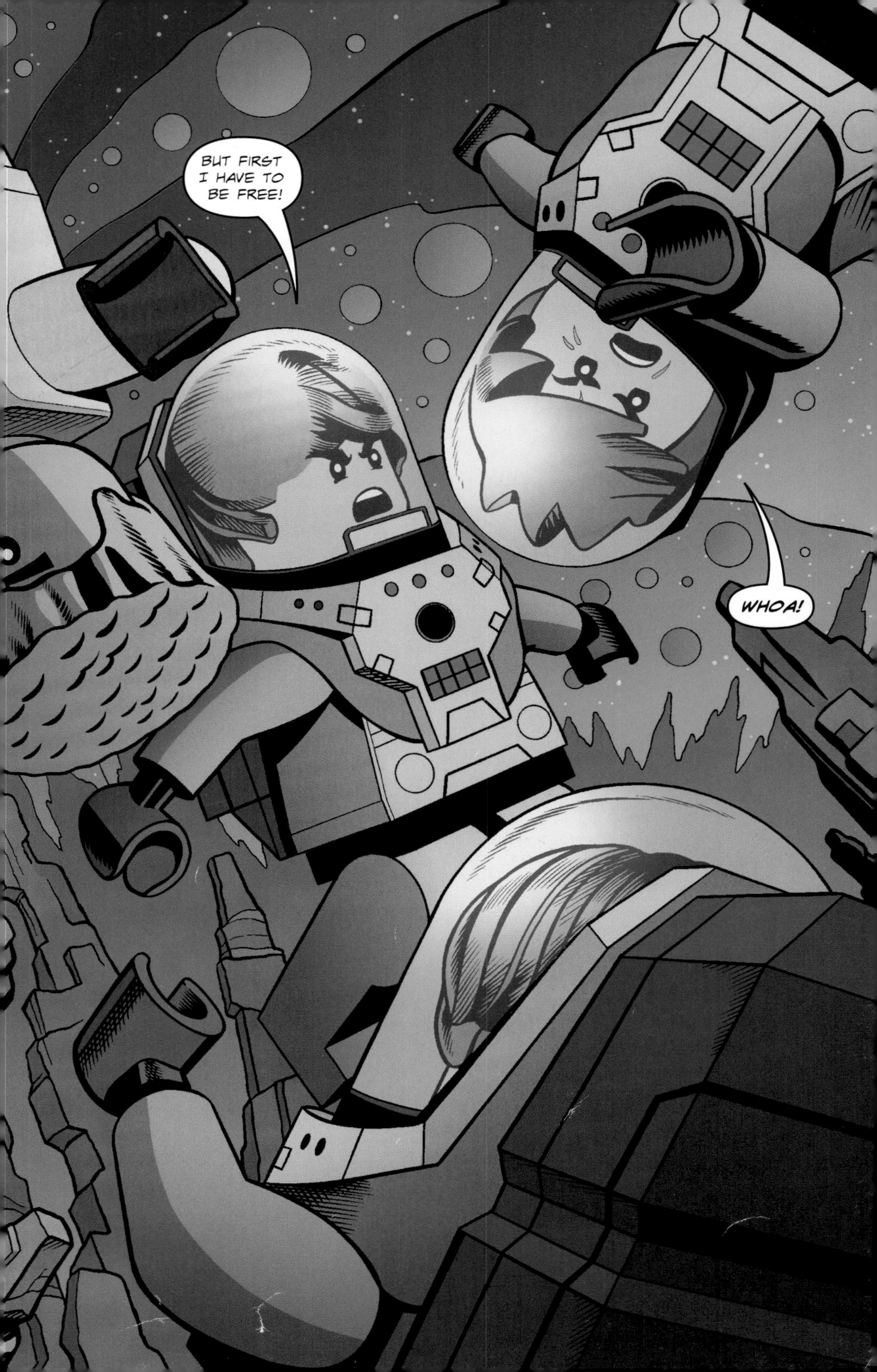
BUT FIRST I HAVE TO BE FREE!
WHOA!

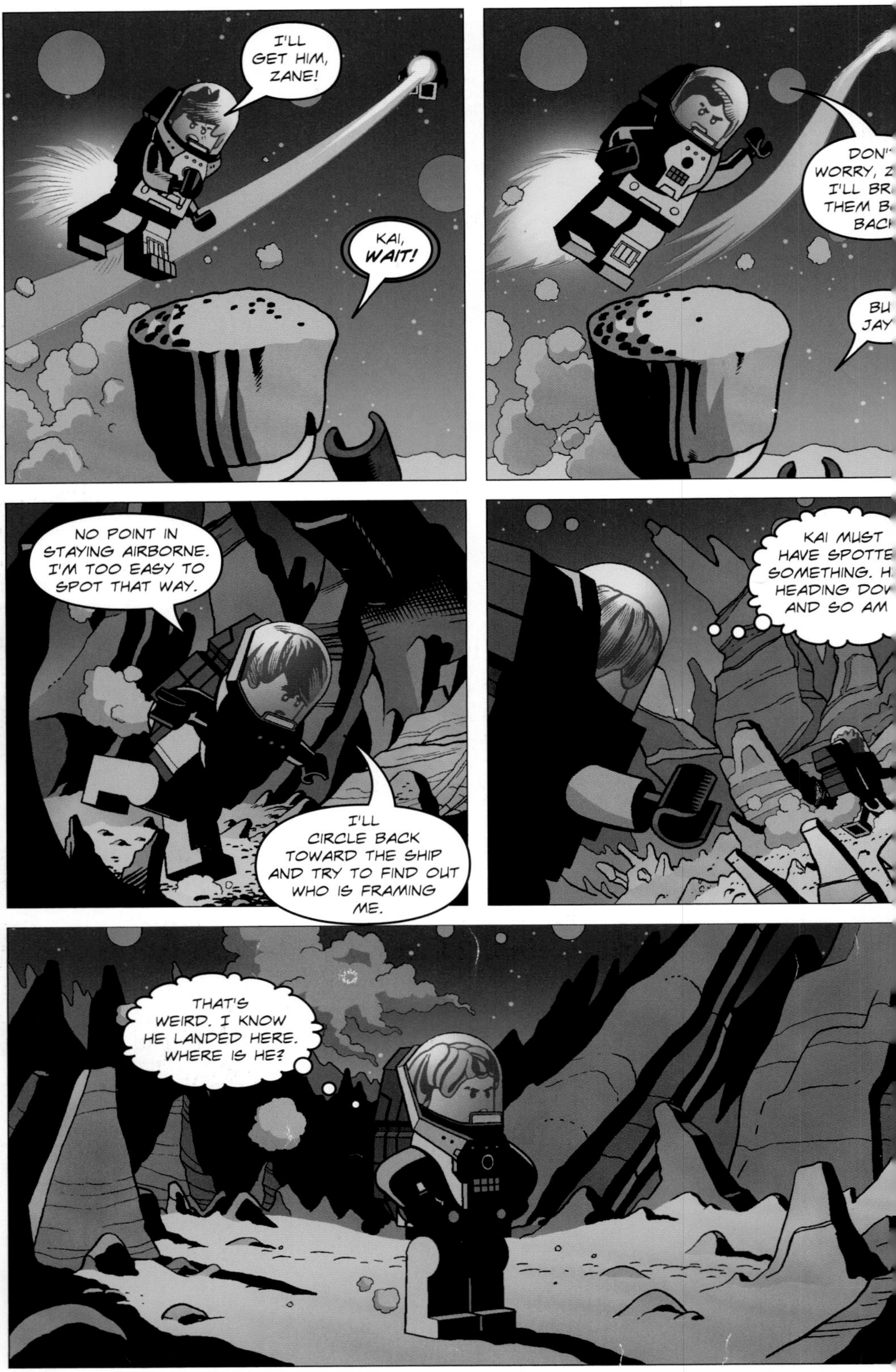
I'LL GET HIM, ZANE!
KAI, WAIT!
DON'T WORRY,
NO POINT IN STAYING AIRBORNE. I'M TOO EASY TO SPOT THAT WAY.
I'LL CIRCLE BACK TOWARD THE SHIP AND TRY TO FIND OUT WHO IS FRAMING ME.
KAI MUST
SOMETHING.
AND SO
THAT'S WEIRD. I KNOW HE LANDED HERE. WHERE IS HE?

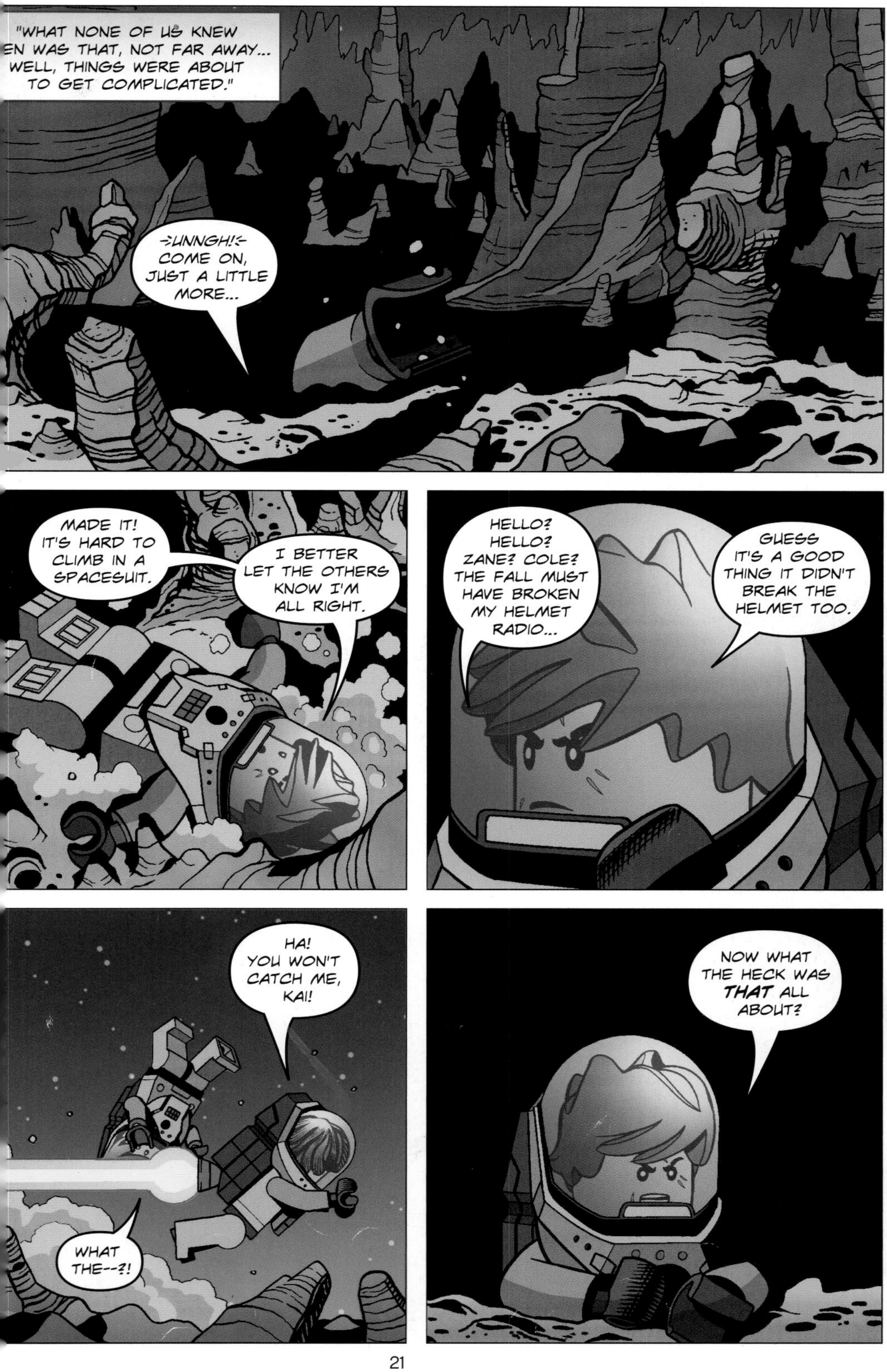
"WHAT NONE OF US KNEW
EN WAS THAT, NOT FAR AWAY...
WELL, THINGS WERE ABOUT
TO GET COMPLICATED."
UNNGH!
COME ON, JUST A LITTLE MORE...
MADE IT! IT'S HARD TO CLIMB IN A SPACESUIT.
I BETTER LET THE OTHERS KNOW I'M ALL RIGHT.
HELLO? HELLO? ZANE? COLE? THE FALL MUST HAVE BROKEN MY HELMET RADIO...
GUESS IT'S A GOOD THING IT DIDN'T BREAK THE HELMET TOO.
HA! YOU WON'T CATCH ME, KAI!
WHAT THE--?!
NOW WHAT THE HECK WAS ***THAT*** ALL ABOUT?

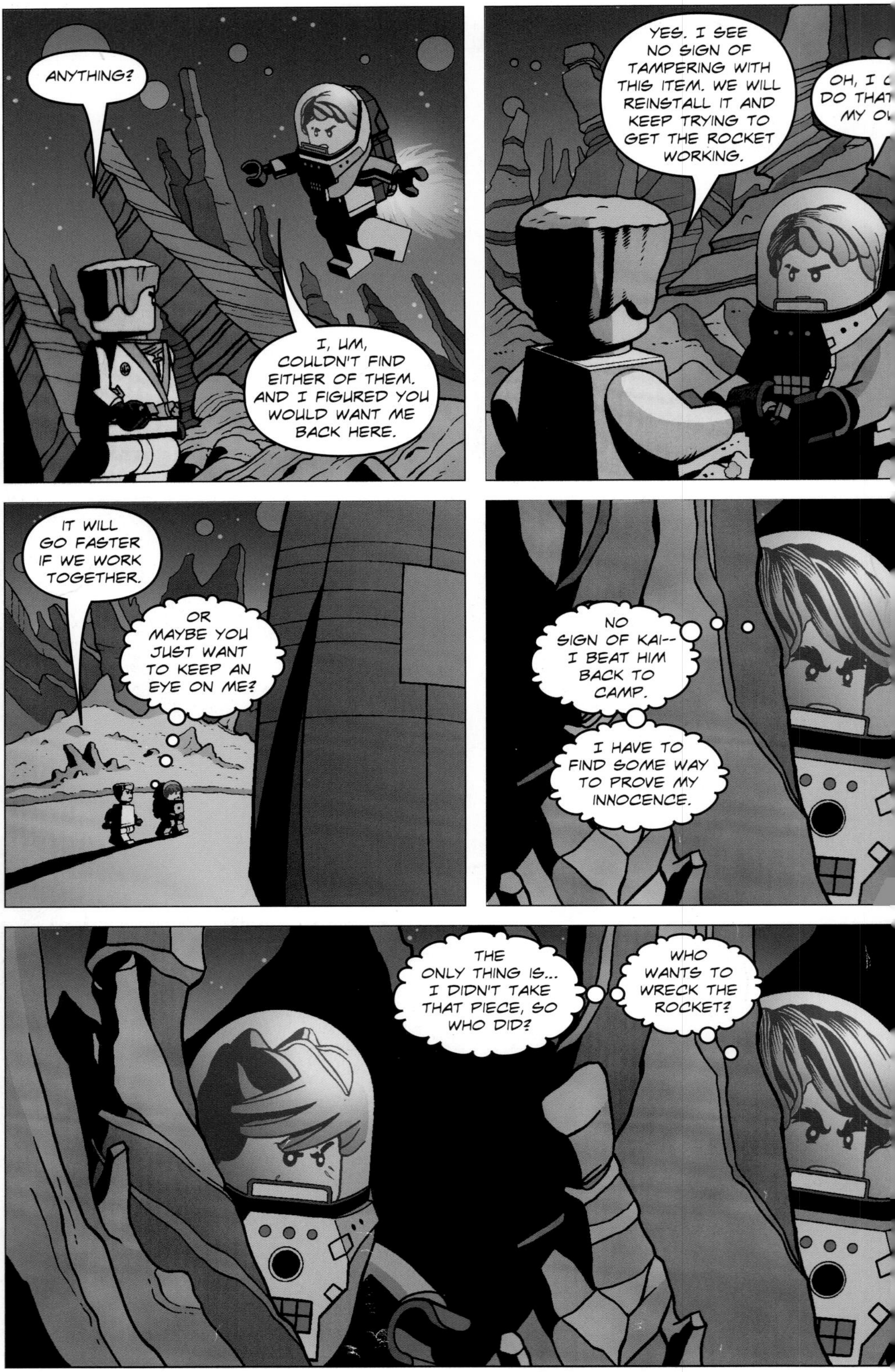
ANYTHING?
I, UM, COULDN'T FIND EITHER OF THEM. AND I FIGURED YOU WOULD WANT ME BACK HERE.
YES. I SEE NO SIGN OF TAMPERING WITH THIS ITEM. WE WILL REINSTALL IT AND KEEP TRYING TO GET THE ROCKET WORKING.
OH, I
DO THAT
MY
IT WILL GO FASTER IF WE WORK TOGETHER.
OR MAYBE YOU JUST WANT TO KEEP AN EYE ON ME?
NO SIGN OF KAI-- I BEAT HIM BACK TO CAMP.
I HAVE TO FIND SOME WAY TO PROVE MY INNOCENCE.
THE ONLY THING IS... I DIDN'T TAKE THAT PIECE, SO WHO DID?
WHO WANTS TO WRECK THE ROCKET?

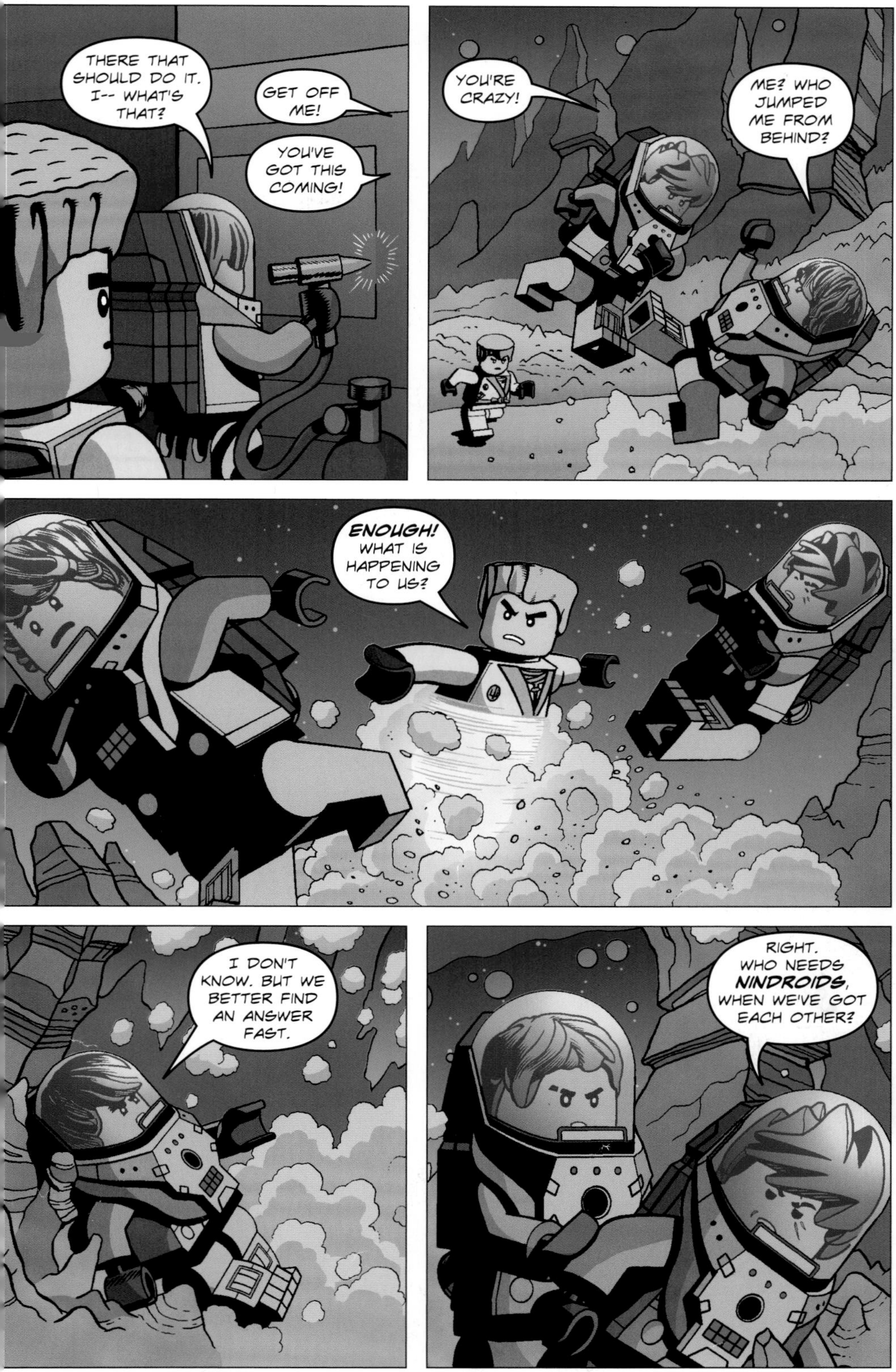
THERE THAT SHOULD DO IT. I-- WHAT'S THAT?
GET OFF ME!
YOU'VE GOT THIS COMING!
YOU'RE CRAZY!
ME? WHO JUMPED ME FROM BEHIND?
ENOUGH! WHAT IS HAPPENING TO US?
I DON'T KNOW. BUT WE BETTER FIND AN ANSWER FAST.
RIGHT. WHO NEEDS NINDROIDS, WHEN WE'VE GOT EACH OTHER?

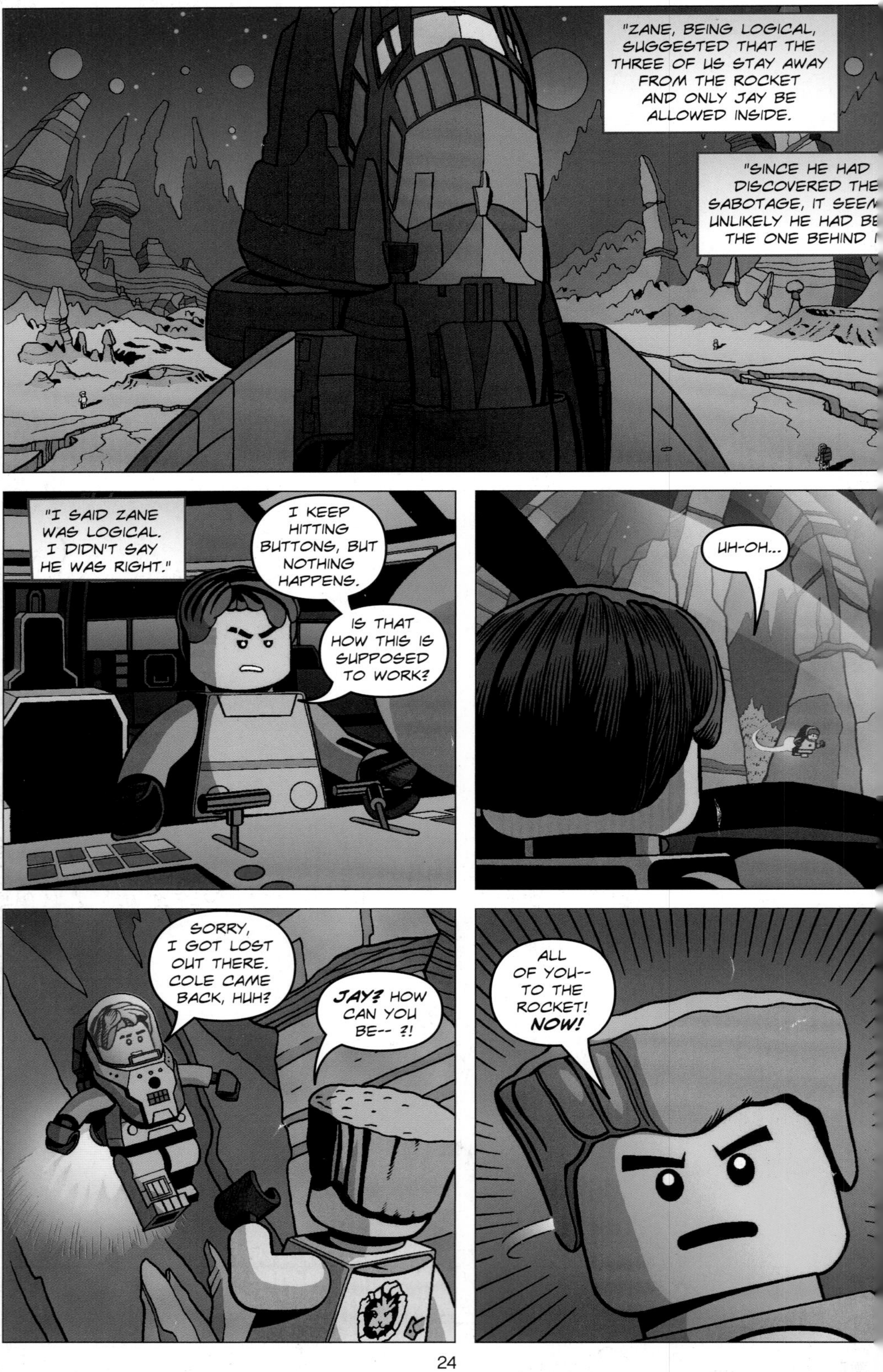
"ZANE, BEING LOGICAL, SUGGESTED THAT THE THREE OF US STAY AWAY FROM THE ROCKET AND ONLY JAY BE ALLOWED INSIDE.
"SINCE HE HAD DISCOVERED THE SABOTAGE, IT SEEM UNLIKELY HE HAD BE THE ONE BEHIND I
"I SAID ZANE WAS LOGICAL. I DIDN'T SAY HE WAS RIGHT."
I KEEP HITTING BUTTONS, BUT NOTHING HAPPENS.
IS THAT HOW THIS IS SUPPOSED TO WORK?
UH-OH...
SORRY, I GOT LOST OUT THERE. COLE CAME BACK, HUH?
JAY? HOW CAN YOU BE-- ?!
ALL OF YOU-- TO THE ROCKET! NOW!

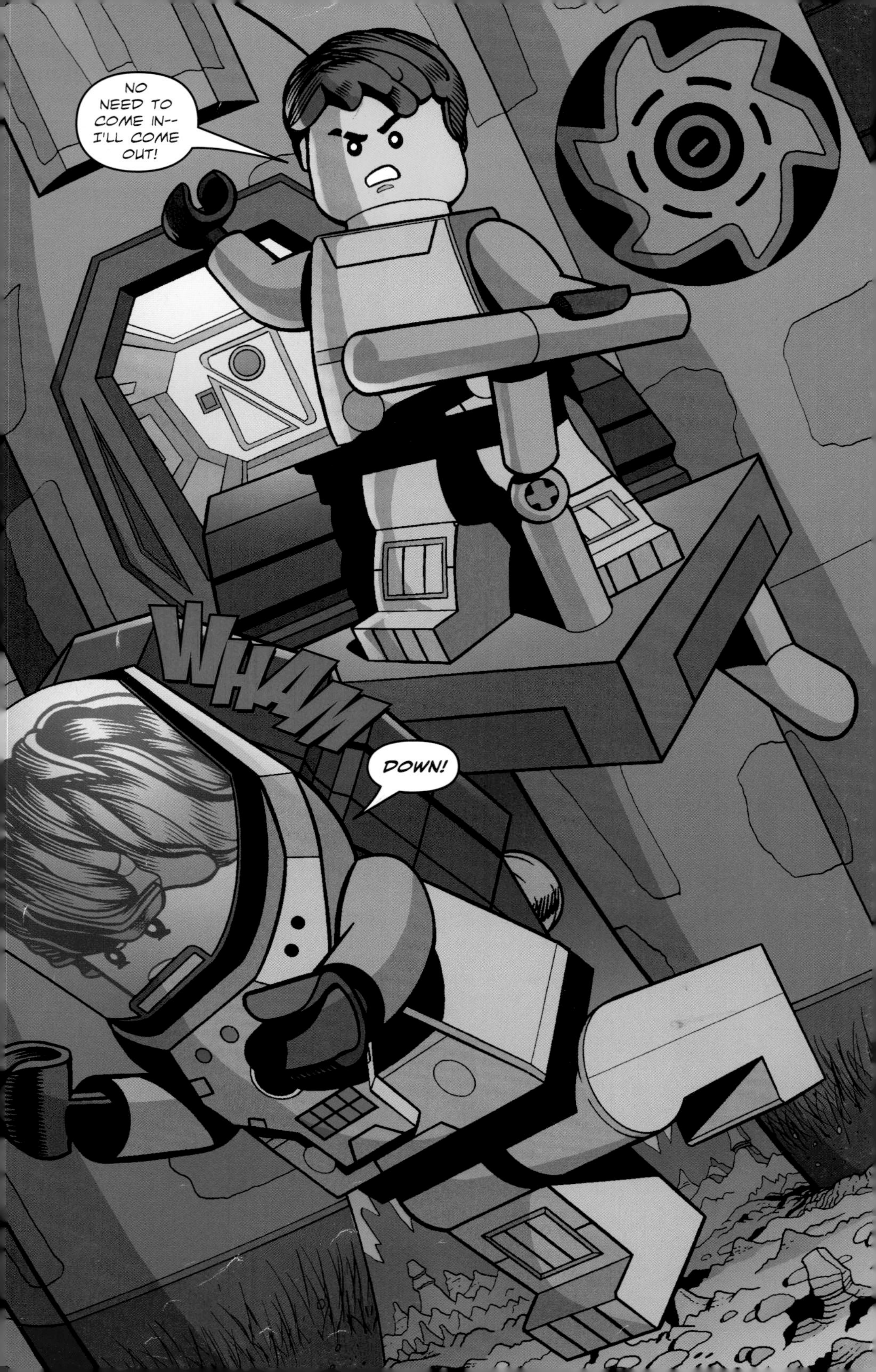
NO NEED TO COME IN-- I'LL COME OUT!
WHAM
DOWN!

AND WHO ARE YOU SUPPOSED TO BE?

NOT ME, I WOULD NEVER BUILD THIS PIECE OF JUNK!

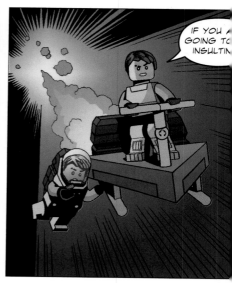

IF YOU A GOING TO INSULTIN

—YOU'LL JUST HAVE TO GET OFF AND WALK.

YIPE.

HEY, IF YOU CRASH THIS THING, WHAT HAPPENS TO YOU?

ME? NOTHING. IN FACT, NOTHING EVER HAPPENS TO ME.

THAT'S THE PROBLEM.

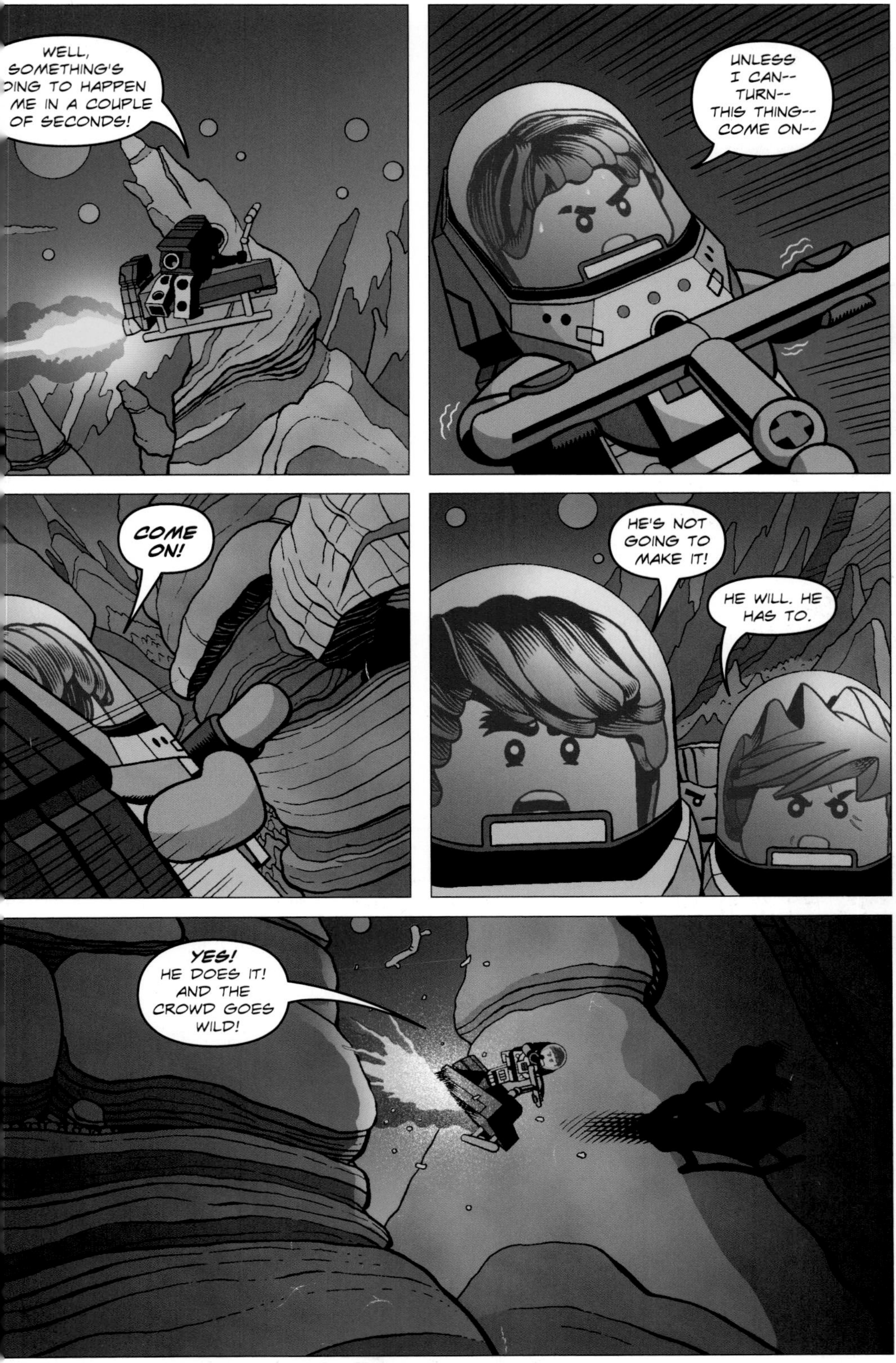
WELL, SOMETHING'S OING TO HAPPEN ME IN A COUPLE OF SECONDS!
UNLESS I CAN-- TURN-- THIS THING-- COME ON--
COME ON!
HE'S NOT GOING TO MAKE IT!
HE WILL. HE HAS TO.
YES! HE DOES IT! AND THE CROWD GOES WILD!

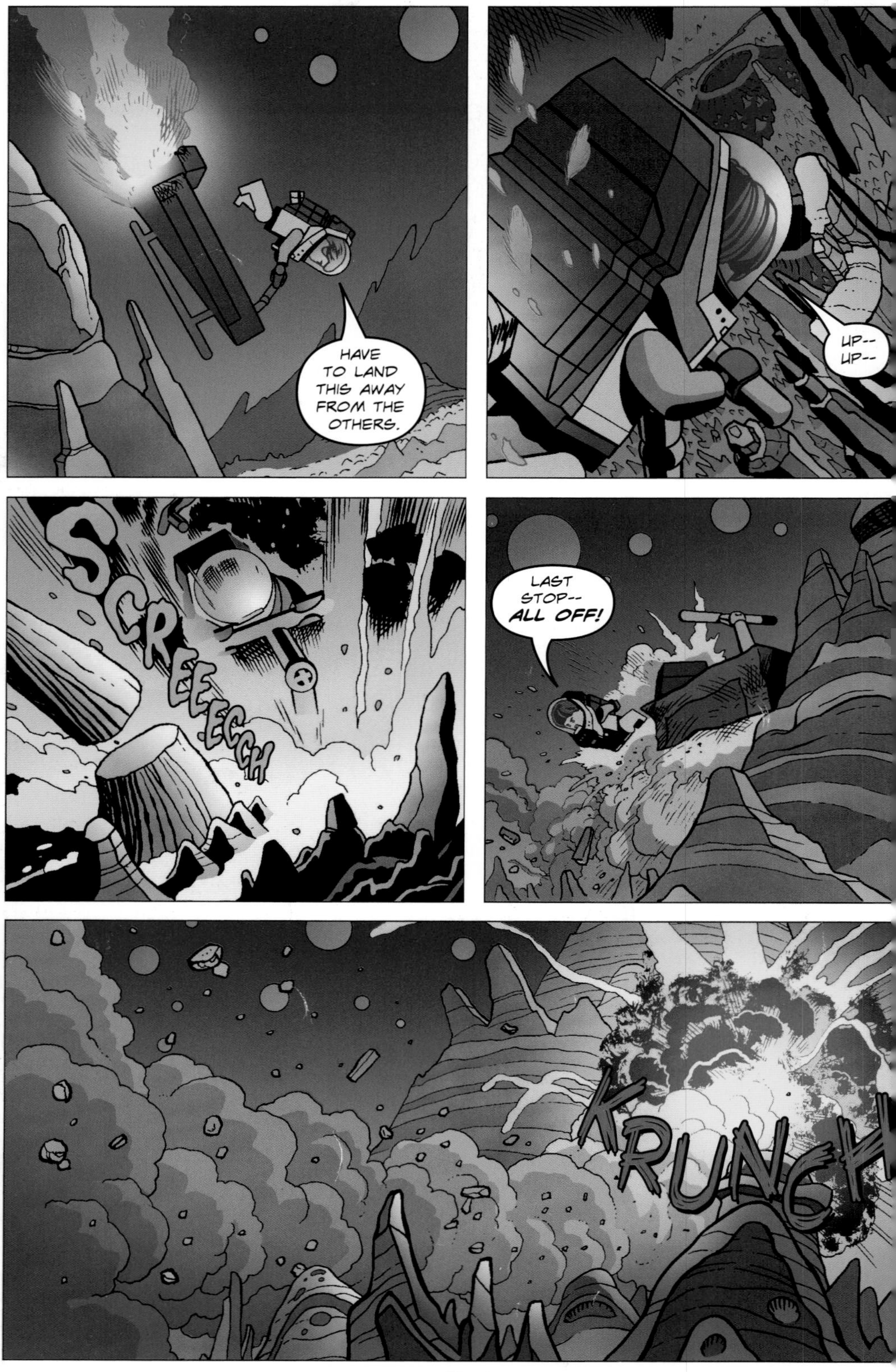
HAVE TO LAND THIS AWAY FROM THE OTHERS.
UP-- UP--
SCREEECCH
LAST STOP-- ALL OFF!
KRUNCH

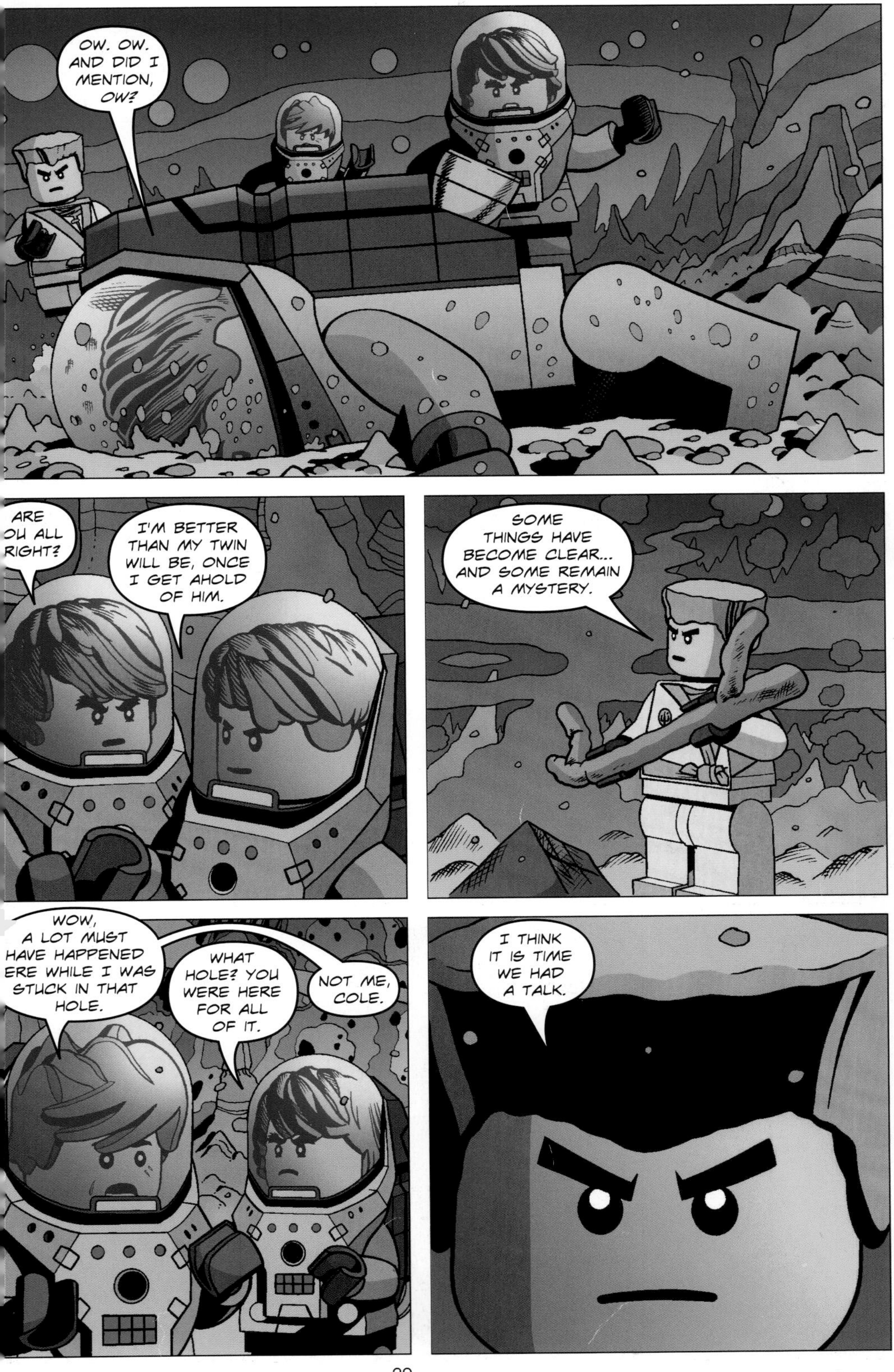
OW. OW. AND DID I MENTION, OW?
ARE OU ALL RIGHT?
I'M BETTER THAN MY TWIN WILL BE, ONCE I GET AHOLD OF HIM.
SOME THINGS HAVE BECOME CLEAR... AND SOME REMAIN A MYSTERY.
WOW, A LOT MUST HAVE HAPPENED ERE WHILE I WAS STUCK IN THAT HOLE.
WHAT HOLE? YOU WERE HERE FOR ALL OF IT.
NOT ME, COLE.
I THINK IT IS TIME WE HAD A TALK.

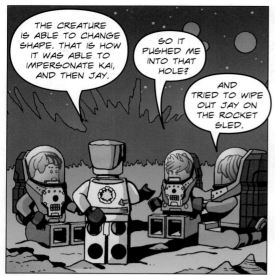

THE CREATURE IS ABLE TO CHANGE SHAPE. THAT IS HOW IT WAS ABLE TO IMPERSONATE KAI, AND THEN JAY.

SO IT PUSHED ME INTO THAT HOLE?

AND TRIED TO WIPE OUT JAY ON THE ROCKET SLED.

MAYBE, MAYBE NOT.

THERE MIGHT HAVE BEEN ENOUGH OF THE REAL JAY IN IT THAT IT KNEW HE COULD ESCAPE.

IT KNEW? I DIDN'T KNOW!

ONE THING WE CAN BE SURE OF:

IT TRIED TO SABOTAGE THE ROCKET.

IT WANTS TO KEEP US HERE.

FROM NOW ON, NONE OF US SHOULD BE ALONE AT ANY TIME.

WOW, ARE WE GOING TO GET TIRED OF EACH OTHER...

HEY, NOBOD COULD E GET TIR OF M

"JAY AND I TOOK FIRST WATCH. E WAS MEDITATING IN THE ROCKET, ND KAI WAS IN THERE SLEEPING... BUT JAY WAS THE ONE ABOUT TO HAVE A NIGHTMARE."

COLE, IS THAT YOU?

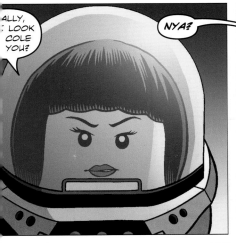

ALLY, LOOK COLE YOU?

NYA?

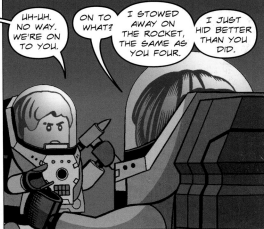

UH-UH. NO WAY. WE'RE ON TO YOU.

ON TO WHAT?

I STOWED AWAY ON THE ROCKET, THE SAME AS YOU FOUR.

I JUST HID BETTER THAN YOU DID.

JUST BACK OFF.

NOW I SUPPOSE YOU WANT TO GET BACK INTO THE COCKPIT, RIGHT?

NO. I CAME BECAUSE I FINALLY DECIDED WHO I LIKE BETTER, COLE OR YOU.

31

HUH? WHAT DID YOU SAY?

THAT'S RIGHT. I LIKE COLE MUCH BETTER.

WHY DO YOU THINK I WOULD WASTE MY TIME ON A CLOWN LIKE YOU?

ZANE'S MORE FUN THAN YOU ARE, AND HE'S A MACHINE.

HEY, COME ON, YOU CAN'T MEAN THAT.

I'M WAY MORE FUN THAN ZANE, ASK ANYBODY!

YOU WERE GOOD FOR A FEW LAUGHS, BUT THAT'S ALL.

YOU KNOW YOU CAN'T COMPETE WITH SOMEONE LIKE COLE.

GET AWAY FROM ME. I'M NOT TALKING TO YOU ANYMORE.

WELL, YOU'RE RIG ABOUT TH ANYWAY

ZANE, I GOT AN IDEA FOR HOW TO FIX THE SHIP!

TAKE THE REST OF MY WATCH WITH COLE AND I'LL HAVE THIS THING UP AND RUNNING IN NO TIME.

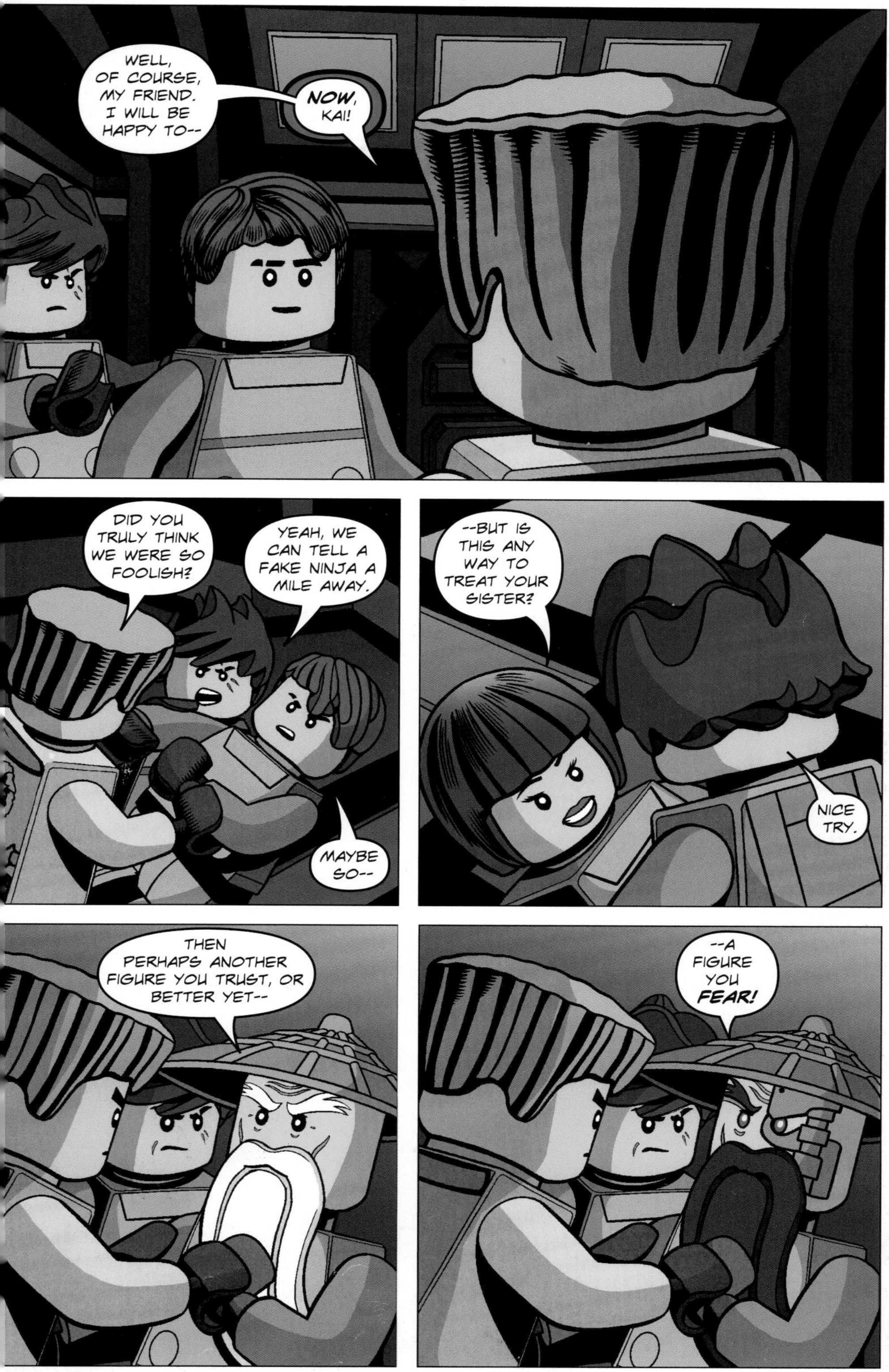
WELL, OF COURSE, MY FRIEND. I WILL BE HAPPY TO--
NOW, KAI!
DID YOU TRULY THINK WE WERE SO FOOLISH?
YEAH, WE CAN TELL A FAKE NINJA A MILE AWAY.
MAYBE SO--
--BUT IS THIS ANY WAY TO TREAT YOUR SISTER?
NICE TRY.
THEN PERHAPS ANOTHER FIGURE YOU TRUST, OR BETTER YET--
--A FIGURE YOU FEAR!

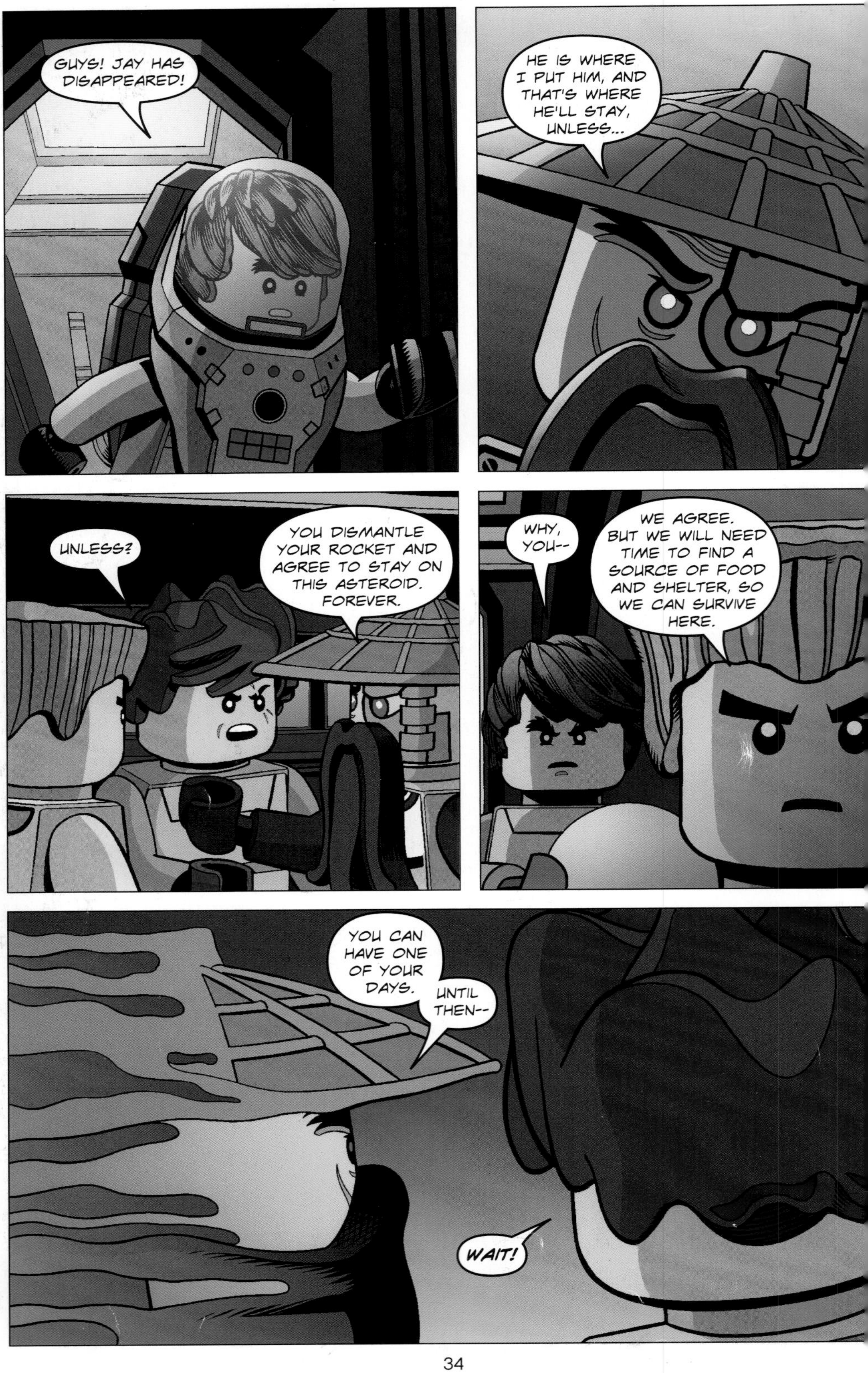
GUYS! JAY HAS DISAPPEARED!
HE IS WHERE I PUT HIM, AND THAT'S WHERE HE'LL STAY, UNLESS...
UNLESS?
YOU DISMANTLE YOUR ROCKET AND AGREE TO STAY ON THIS ASTEROID. FOREVER.
WHY, YOU--
WE AGREE. BUT WE WILL NEED TIME TO FIND A SOURCE OF FOOD AND SHELTER, SO WE CAN SURVIVE HERE.
YOU CAN HAVE ONE OF YOUR DAYS.
UNTIL THEN--
WAIT!

USE YOUR TIME WISELY.

OH, WE WILL. WE HAVE 24 HOURS TO FIND JAY. LET'S GET MOVING.

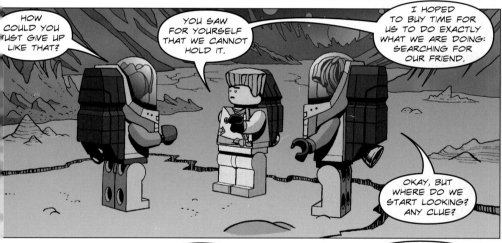

HOW COULD YOU JUST GIVE UP LIKE THAT?

YOU SAW FOR YOURSELF THAT WE CANNOT HOLD IT.

I HOPED TO BUY TIME FOR US TO DO EXACTLY WHAT WE ARE DOING: SEARCHING FOR OUR FRIEND.

OKAY, BUT WHERE DO WE START LOOKING? ANY CLUE?

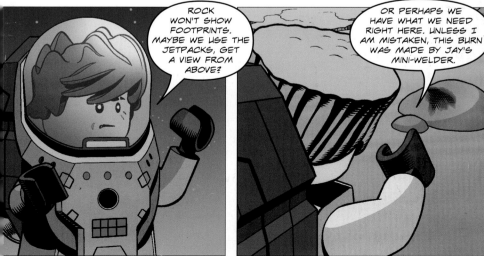

ROCK WON'T SHOW FOOTPRINTS. MAYBE WE USE THE JETPACKS, GET A VIEW FROM ABOVE?

OR PERHAPS WE HAVE WHAT WE NEED RIGHT HERE. UNLESS I AM MISTAKEN, THIS BURN WAS MADE BY JAY'S MINI-WELDER.

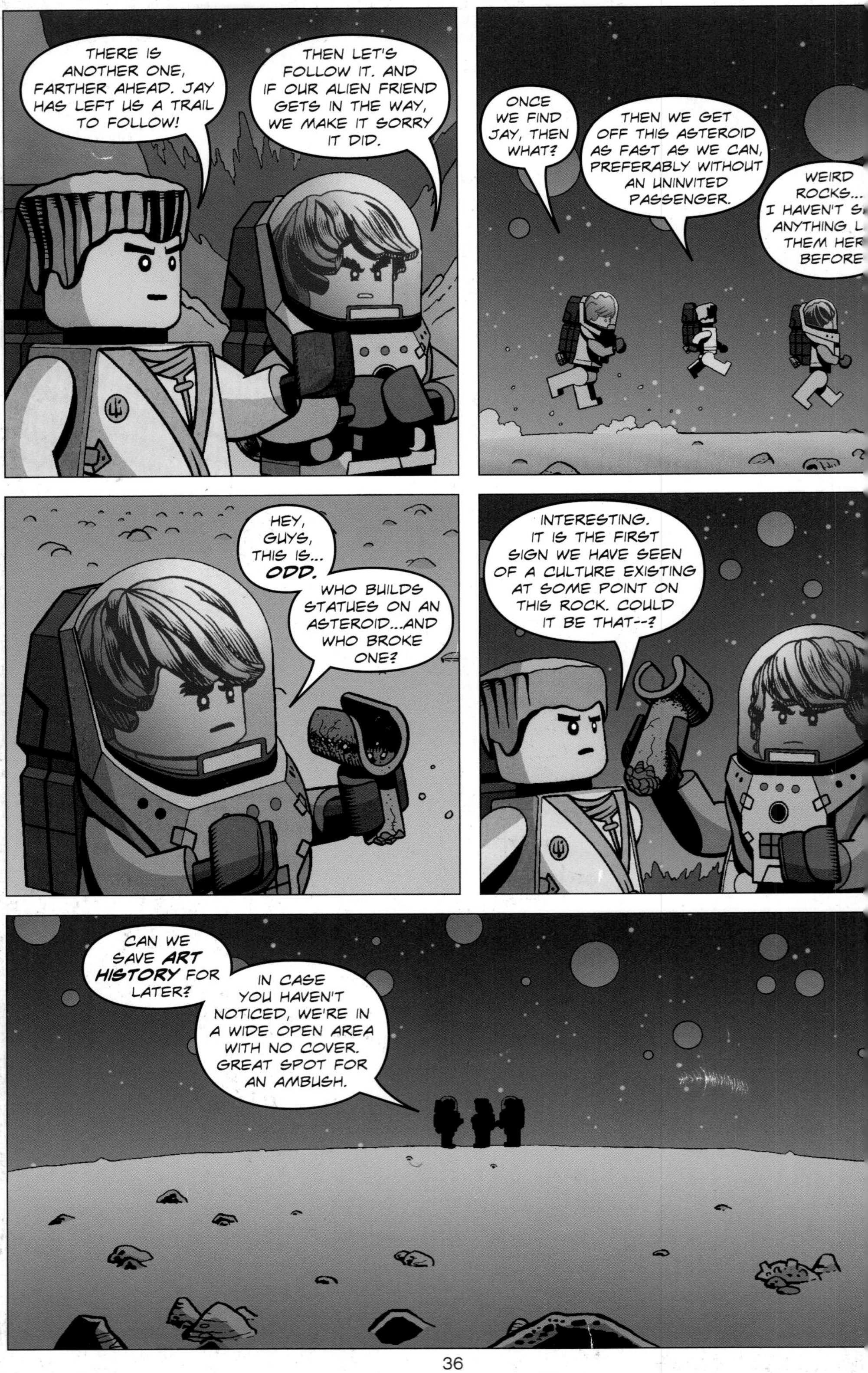
THERE IS ANOTHER ONE, FARTHER AHEAD. JAY HAS LEFT US A TRAIL TO FOLLOW!
THEN LET'S FOLLOW IT. AND IF OUR ALIEN FRIEND GETS IN THE WAY, WE MAKE IT SORRY IT DID.
ONCE WE FIND JAY, THEN WHAT?
THEN WE GET OFF THIS ASTEROID AS FAST AS WE CAN, PREFERABLY WITHOUT AN UNINVITED PASSENGER.
WEIRD ROCKS... I HAVEN'T S ANYTHING L THEM HER BEFORE
HEY, GUYS, THIS IS... **ODD.**
WHO BUILDS STATUES ON AN ASTEROID...AND WHO BROKE ONE?
INTERESTING. IT IS THE FIRST SIGN WE HAVE SEEN OF A CULTURE EXISTING AT SOME POINT ON THIS ROCK. COULD IT BE THAT--?
CAN WE SAVE **ART HISTORY** FOR LATER?
IN CASE YOU HAVEN'T NOTICED, WE'RE IN A WIDE OPEN AREA WITH NO COVER. GREAT SPOT FOR AN AMBUSH.

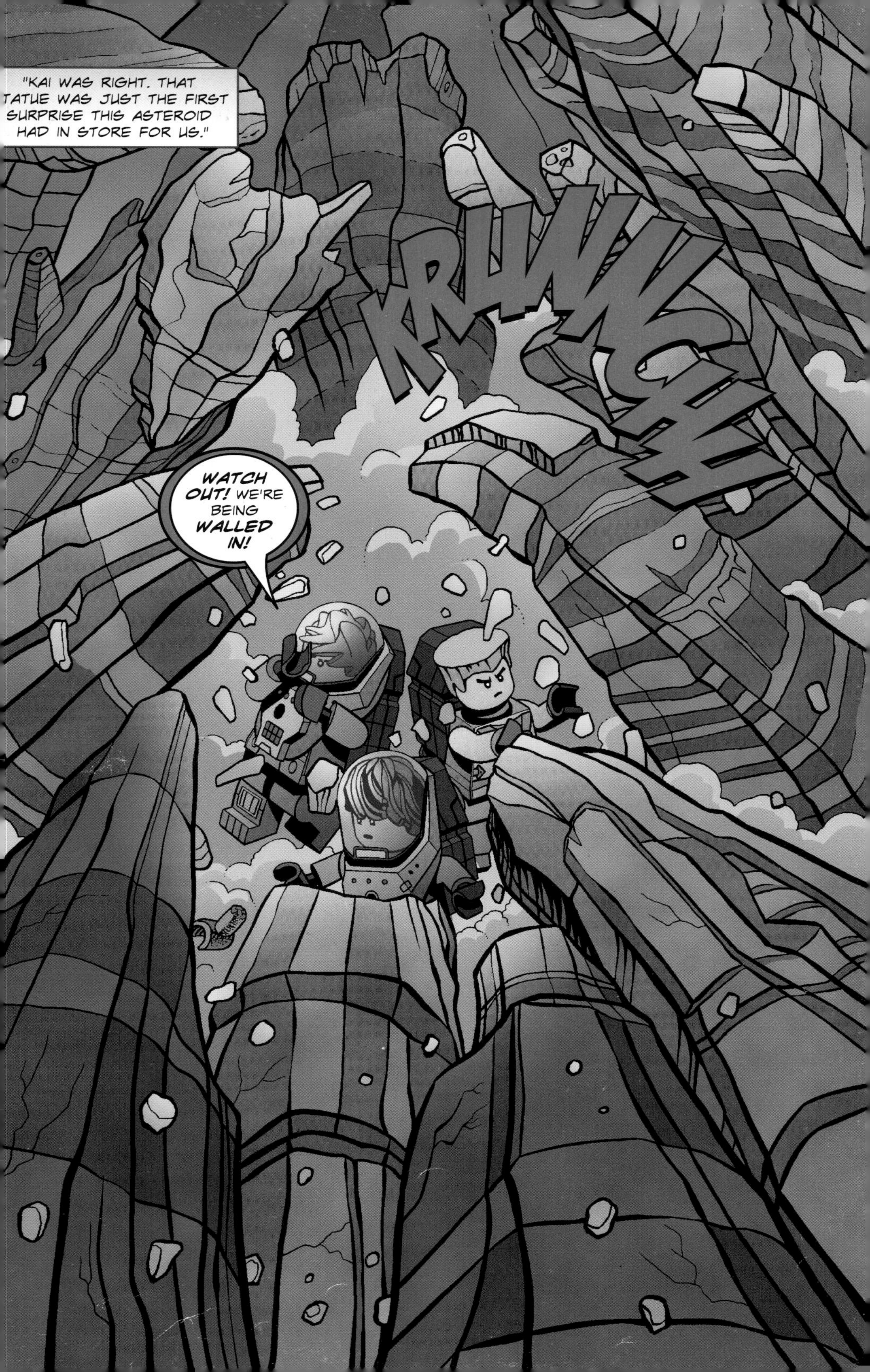
"KAI WAS RIGHT. THAT
TATUE WAS JUST THE FIRST
SURPRISE THIS ASTEROID
HAD IN STORE FOR US."
KRUNNCHH
WATCH OUT! WE'RE BEING WALLED IN!

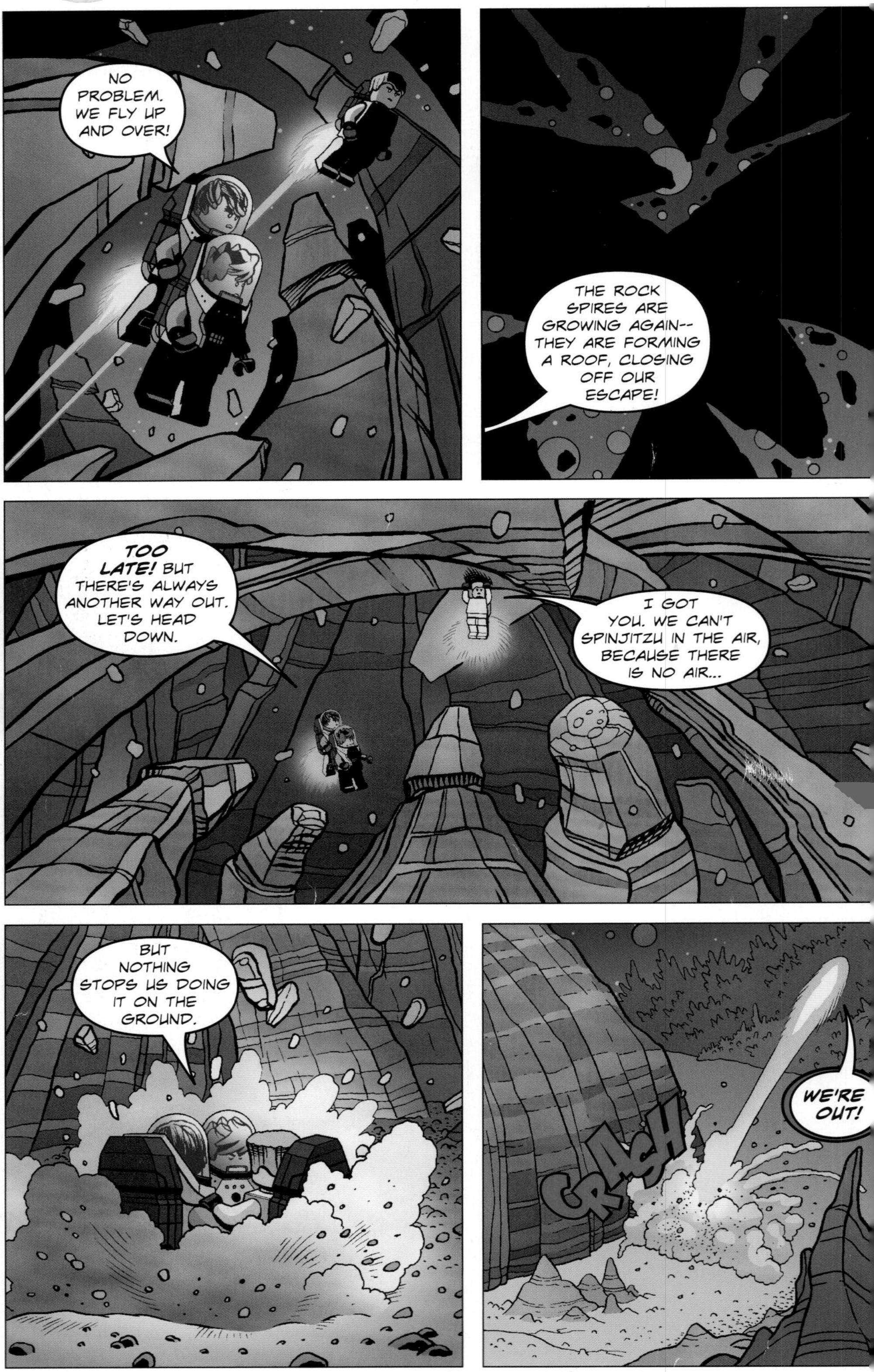
NO PROBLEM. WE FLY UP AND OVER!
THE ROCK SPIRES ARE GROWING AGAIN-- THEY ARE FORMING A ROOF, CLOSING OFF OUR ESCAPE!
TOO LATE! BUT THERE'S ALWAYS ANOTHER WAY OUT. LET'S HEAD DOWN.
I GOT YOU. WE CAN'T SPINJITZU IN THE AIR, BECAUSE THERE IS NO AIR...
BUT NOTHING STOPS US DOING IT ON THE GROUND.
CRASH
WE'RE OUT!

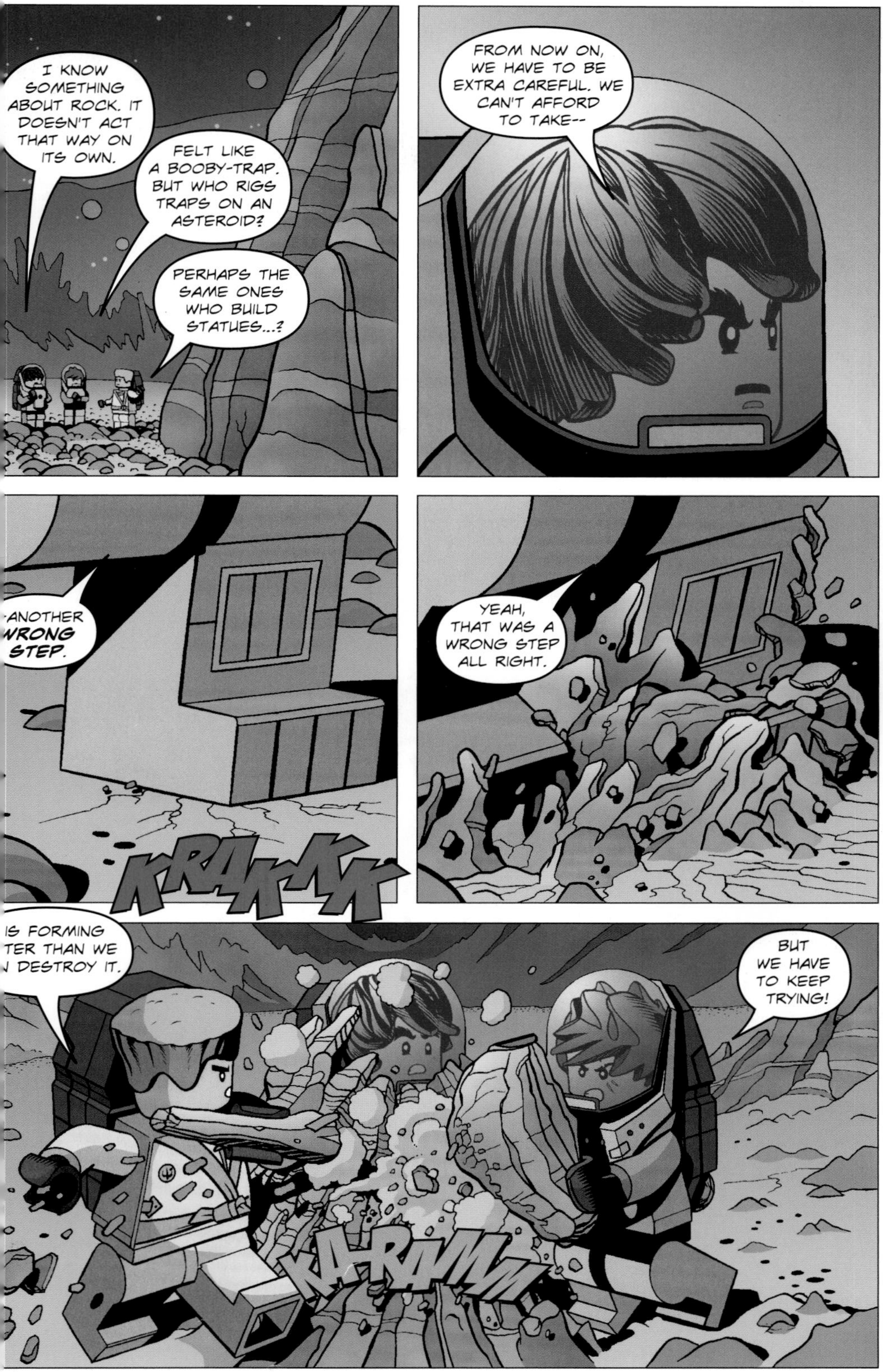
I KNOW SOMETHING ABOUT ROCK. IT DOESN'T ACT THAT WAY ON ITS OWN.
FELT LIKE A BOOBY-TRAP. BUT WHO RIGS TRAPS ON AN ASTEROID?
PERHAPS THE SAME ONES WHO BUILD STATUES...?
FROM NOW ON, WE HAVE TO BE EXTRA CAREFUL. WE CAN'T AFFORD TO TAKE--
ANOTHER
RONG STEP.
KRAKKK
YEAH, THAT WAS A WRONG STEP ALL RIGHT.
IS FORMING
TER THAN WE
N DESTROY IT.
BUT WE HAVE TO KEEP TRYING!
KA-RAMM

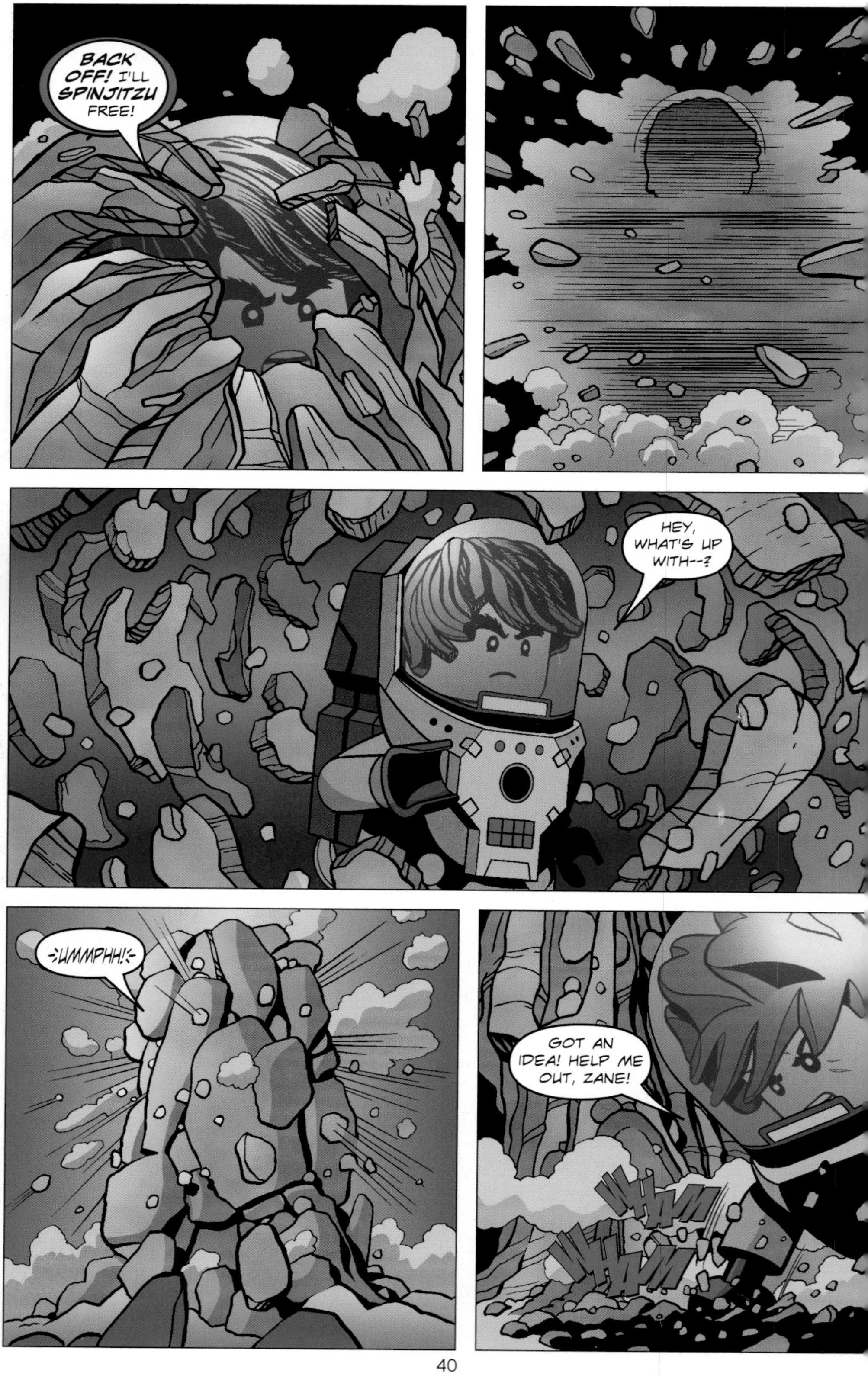
BACK OFF! I'LL SPINJITZU FREE!
HEY, WHAT'S UP WITH--?
UMMPHH!
GOT AN IDEA! HELP ME OUT, ZANE!
WHAM
WHAM

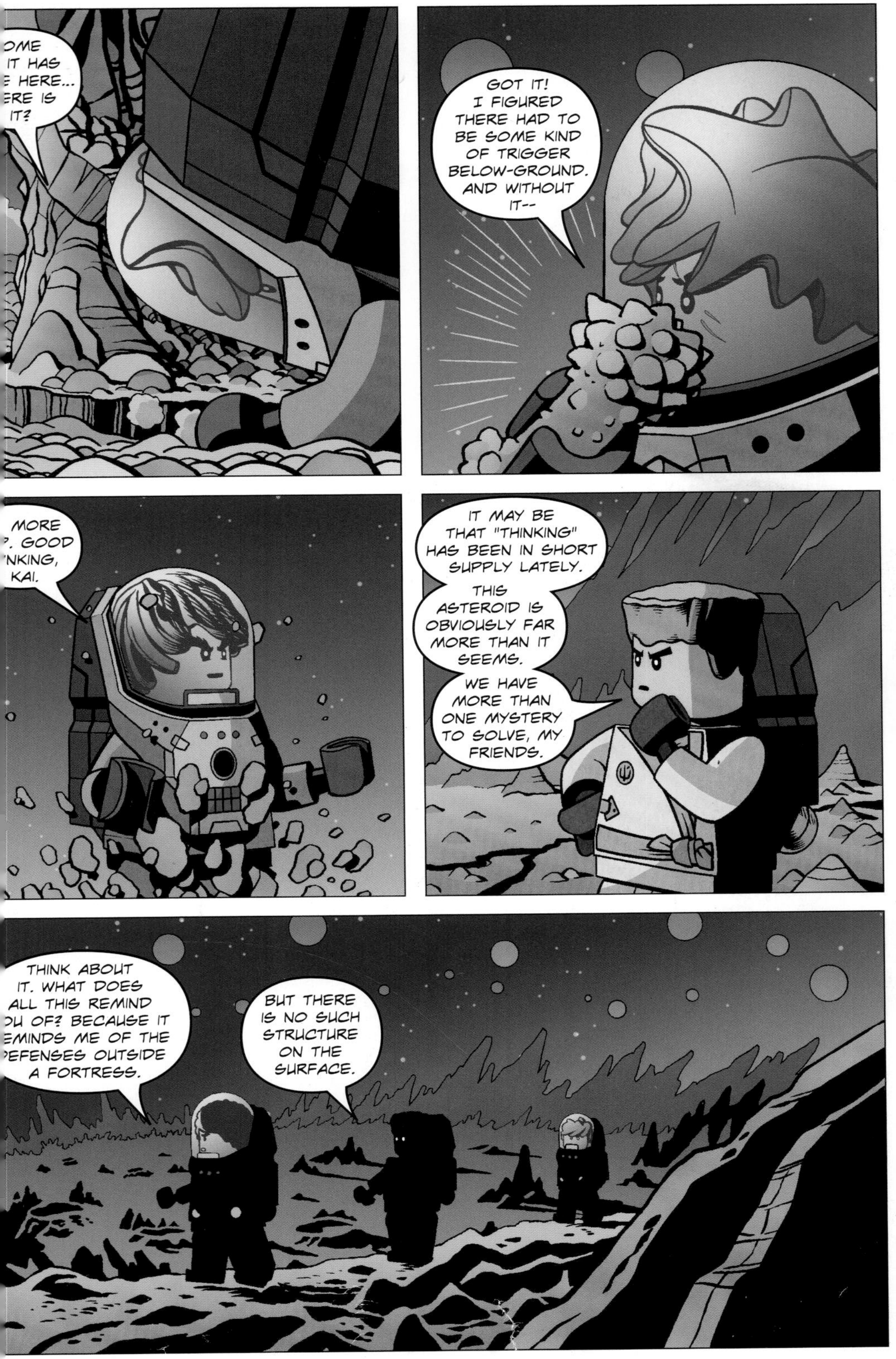
OME IT HAS E HERE... ERE IS IT?
GOT IT! I FIGURED THERE HAD TO BE SOME KIND OF TRIGGER BELOW-GROUND. AND WITHOUT IT--
MORE ?. GOOD NKING, KAI.
IT MAY BE THAT "THINKING" HAS BEEN IN SHORT SUPPLY LATELY.
THIS ASTEROID IS OBVIOUSLY FAR MORE THAN IT SEEMS.
WE HAVE MORE THAN ONE MYSTERY TO SOLVE, MY FRIENDS.
THINK ABOUT IT. WHAT DOES ALL THIS REMIND OU OF? BECAUSE IT EMINDS ME OF THE EFENSES OUTSIDE A FORTRESS.
BUT THERE IS NO SUCH STRUCTURE ON THE SURFACE.

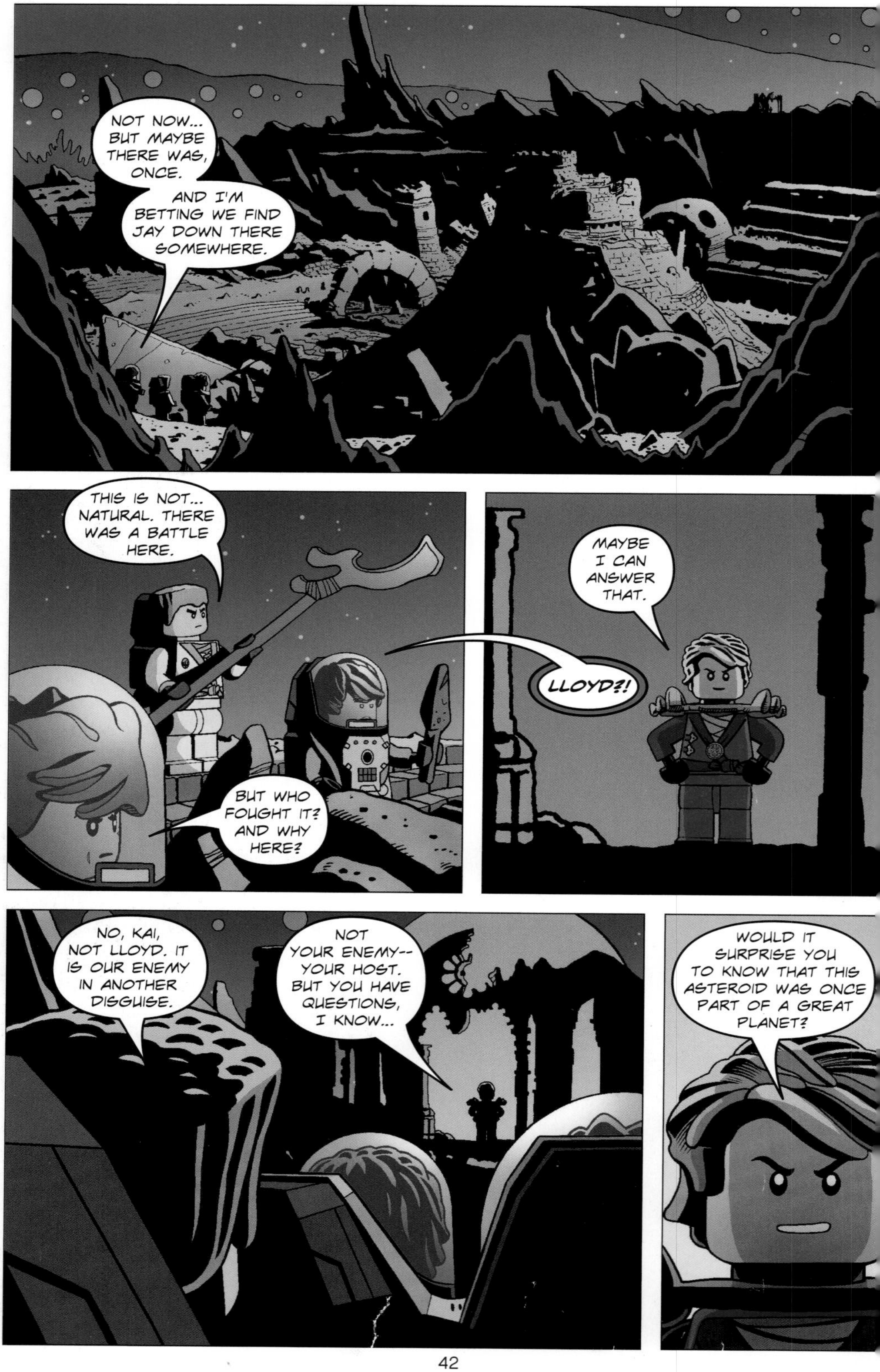
NOT NOW... BUT MAYBE THERE WAS, ONCE.
AND I'M BETTING WE FIND JAY DOWN THERE SOMEWHERE.
THIS IS NOT... NATURAL. THERE WAS A BATTLE HERE.
BUT WHO FOUGHT IT? AND WHY HERE?
MAYBE I CAN ANSWER THAT.
LLOYD?!
NO, KAI, NOT LLOYD. IT IS OUR ENEMY IN ANOTHER DISGUISE.
NOT YOUR ENEMY-- YOUR HOST. BUT YOU HAVE QUESTIONS, I KNOW...
WOULD IT SURPRISE YOU TO KNOW THAT THIS ASTEROID WAS ONCE PART OF A GREAT PLANET?

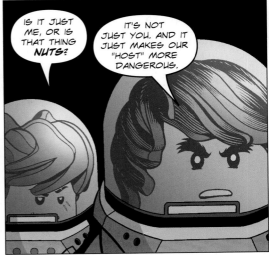

F COURSE
DOESN'T
SURPRISE
US.

IT
SURPRISED
ME.

ME, TOO,
BUT I'M NOT
GOING TO TELL
IT THAT.

IT WAS
QUITE A
NICE PLACE,
TOO...

SHAME
ABOUT IT
BLOWING UP
AND ALL.

DON'T
LET ME
KEEP YOU
FROM WHAT
YOU WERE
DOING.

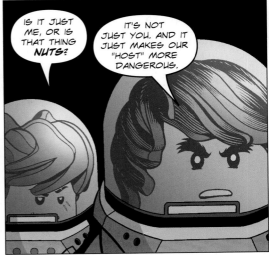
IS IT JUST
ME, OR IS
THAT THING
NUTS?

IT'S NOT
JUST YOU. AND IT
JUST MAKES OUR
"HOST" MORE
DANGEROUS.

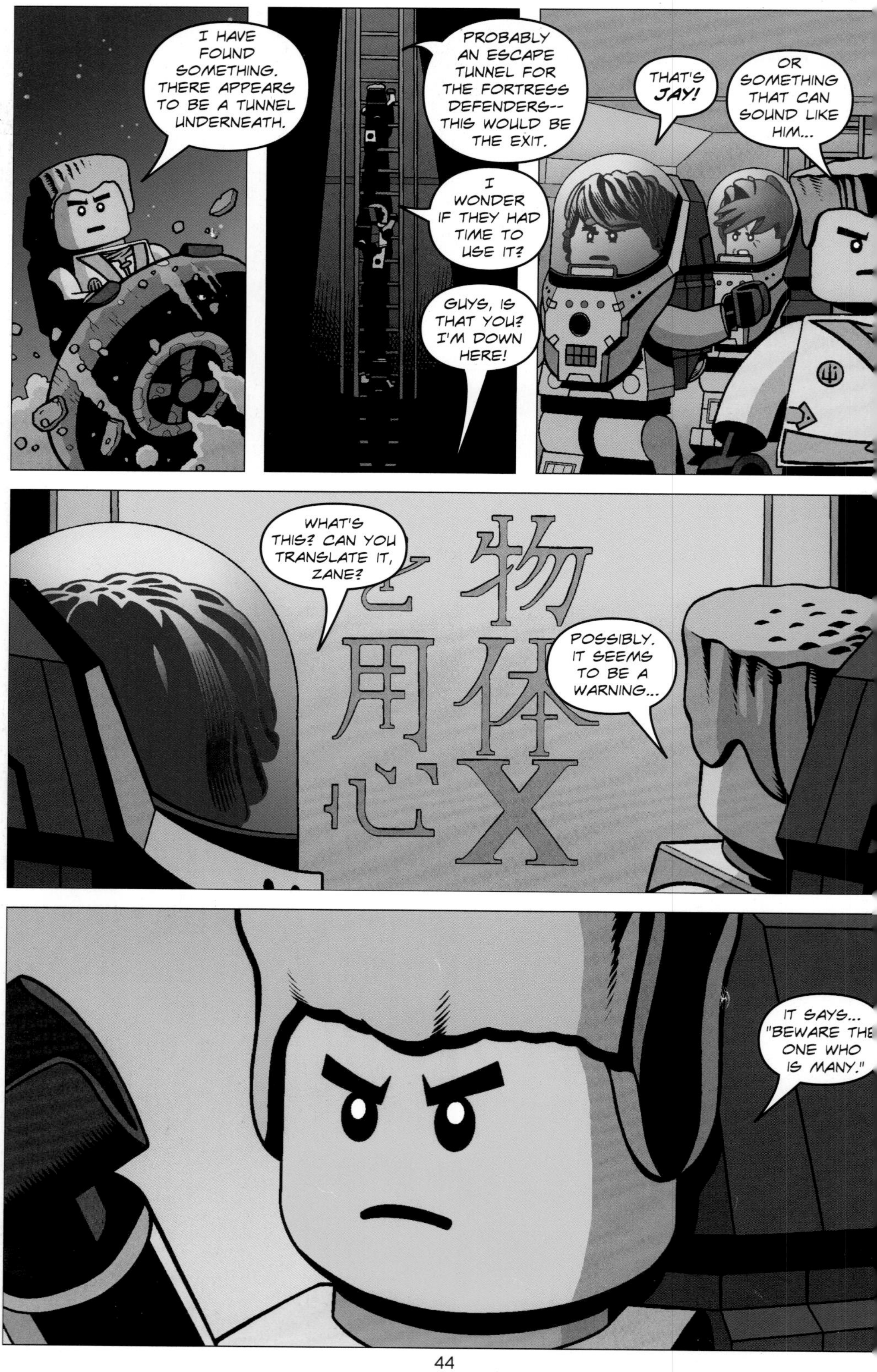
I HAVE FOUND SOMETHING. THERE APPEARS TO BE A TUNNEL UNDERNEATH.
PROBABLY AN ESCAPE TUNNEL FOR THE FORTRESS DEFENDERS-- THIS WOULD BE THE EXIT.
I WONDER IF THEY HAD TIME TO USE IT?
GUYS, IS THAT YOU? I'M DOWN HERE!
THAT'S *JAY!*
OR SOMETHING THAT CAN SOUND LIKE HIM...
WHAT'S THIS? CAN YOU TRANSLATE IT, ZANE?
物体X
用心
POSSIBLY. IT SEEMS TO BE A WARNING...
IT SAYS... "BEWARE THE ONE WHO IS MANY."

GUYS, WHAT ARE YOU WAITING FOR? SOMEBODY UNTIE ME!

THAT DOES IT. JAY OR NOT, I'M GOING TO FIND OUT WHAT'S GOING ON. WHO'S WITH ME?

HEY, WHO TURNED OUT THE LIGHTS?

OH, MAN, NOT THE OLD "USE-THE-LIGHTS-AND-DUPLICATE" TRICK...

YOU SHOULD TALK, YOU'RE THE *PHONY*.

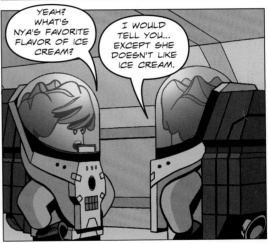

YEAH? WHAT'S NYA'S FAVORITE FLAVOR OF ICE CREAM?

I WOULD TELL YOU... EXCEPT SHE DOESN'T LIKE ICE CREAM.

ZANE-- ?

GIVEN TIME, I COULD TELL THEM APART... I THINK.

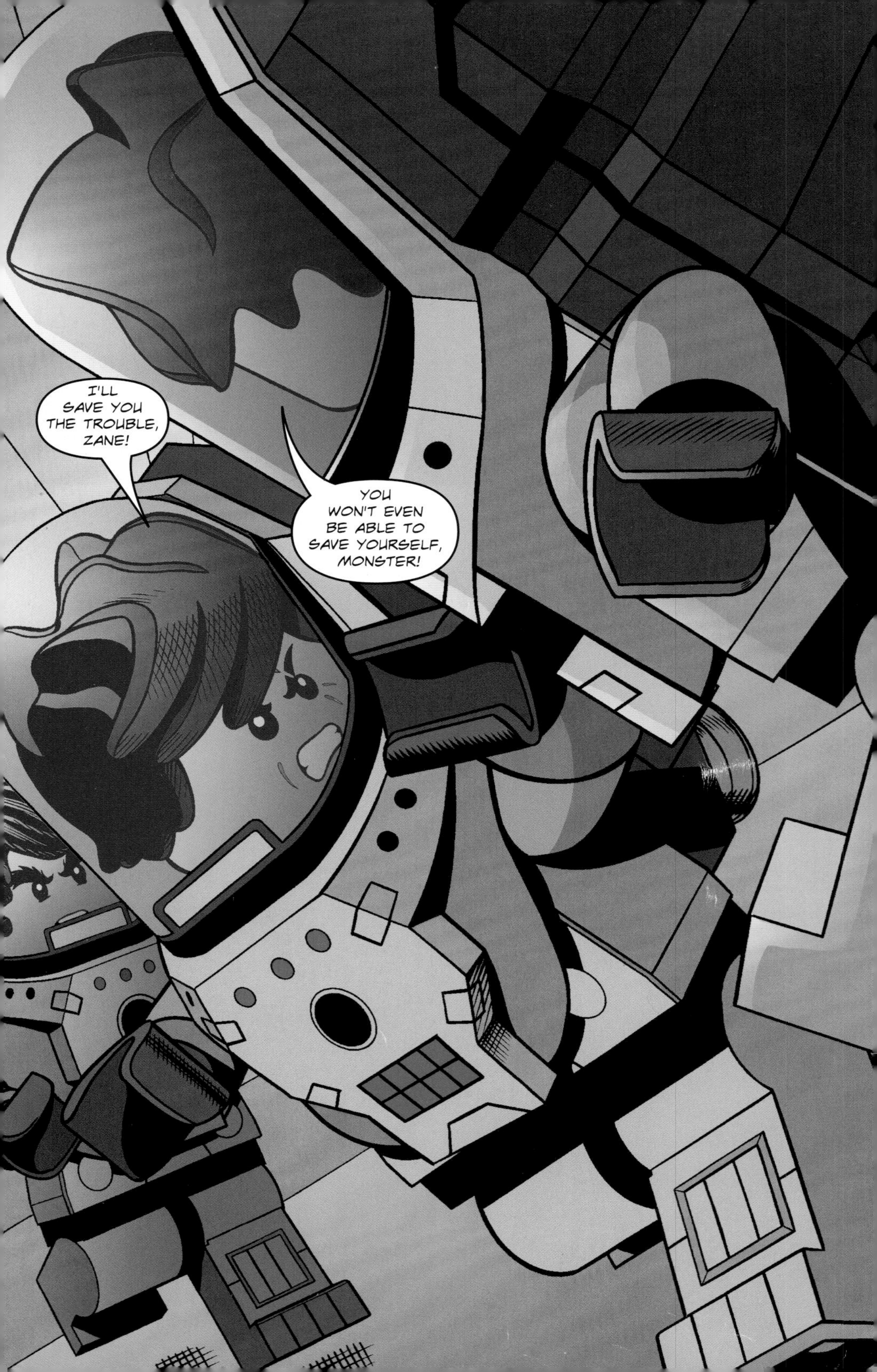
I'LL SAVE YOU THE TROUBLE, ZANE!
YOU WON'T EVEN BE ABLE TO SAVE YOURSELF, MONSTER!

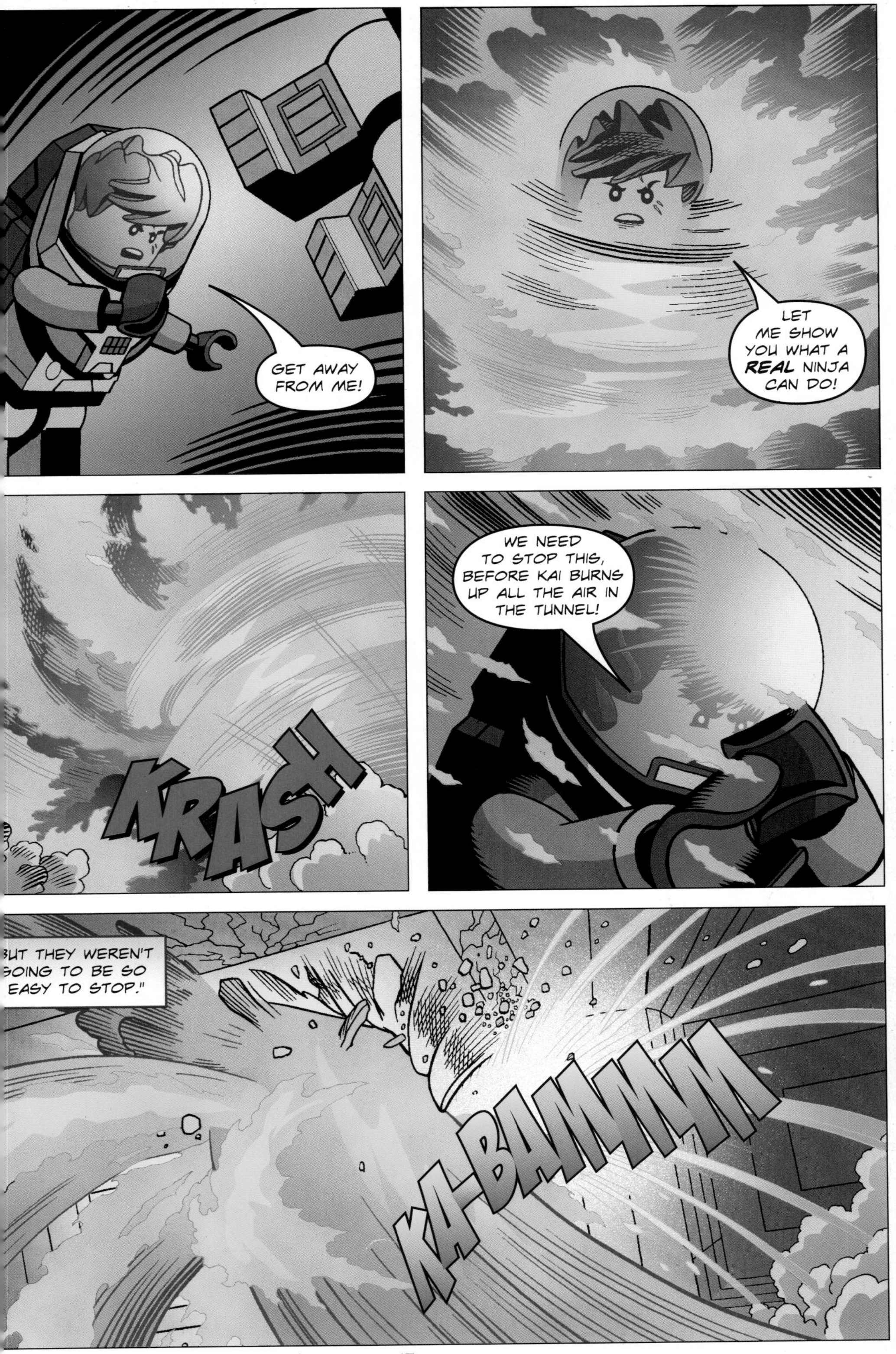
GET AWAY FROM ME!
LET ME SHOW YOU WHAT A REAL NINJA CAN DO!
KRASH
WE NEED TO STOP THIS, BEFORE KAI BURNS UP ALL THE AIR IN THE TUNNEL!
BUT THEY WEREN'T GOING TO BE SO EASY TO STOP."
KA-BAMMMM

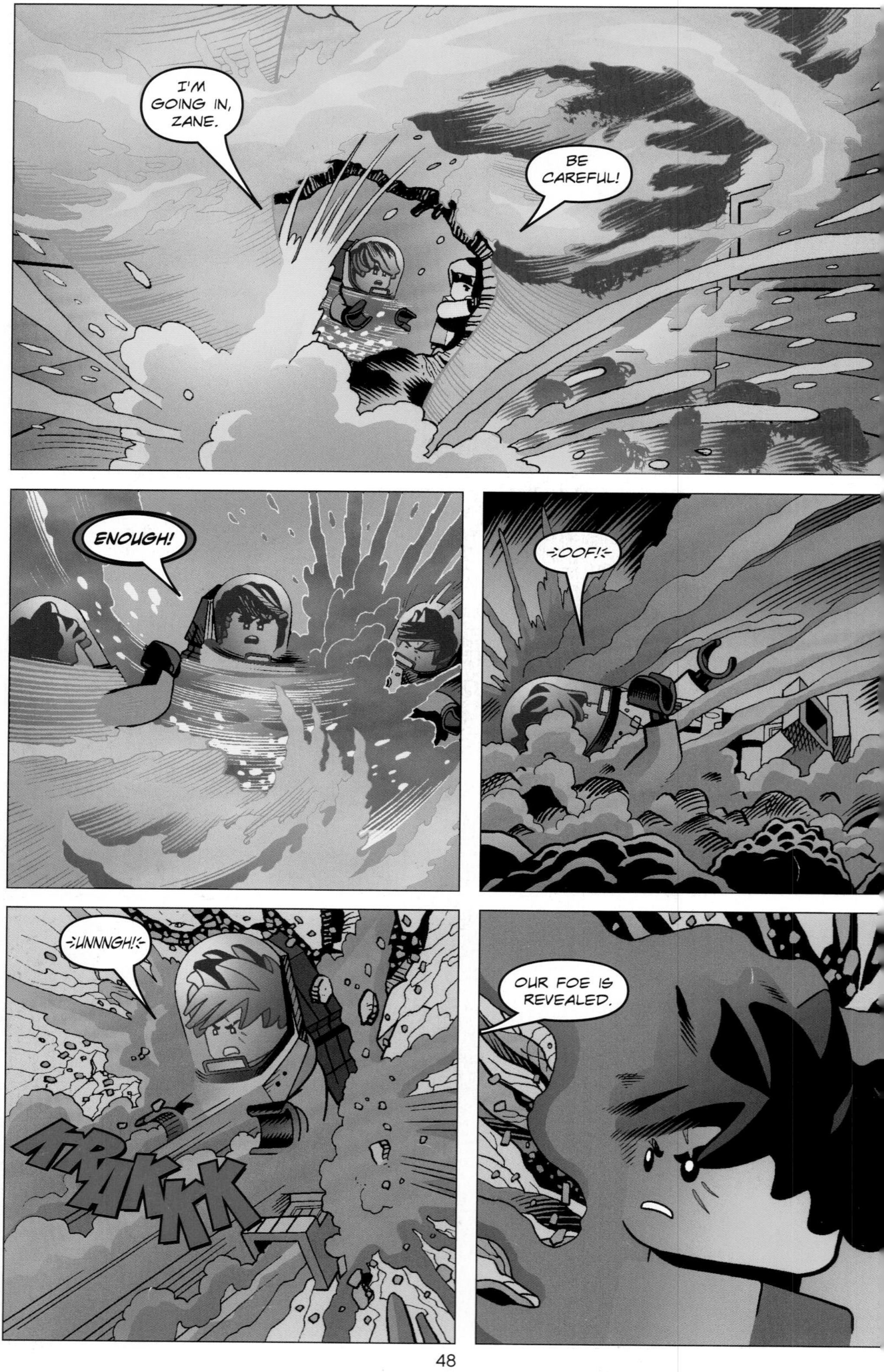
I'M GOING IN, ZANE.
BE CAREFUL!
ENOUGH!
-OOF!-
-UNNNGH!-
KRAKKK
OUR FOE IS REVEALED.

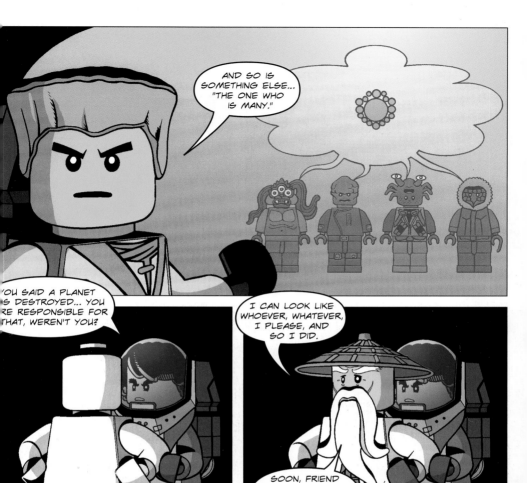

AND SO IS SOMETHING ELSE... "THE ONE WHO IS MANY."

YOU SAID A PLANET IS DESTROYED... YOU RE RESPONSIBLE FOR THAT, WEREN'T YOU?

I CAN LOOK LIKE WHOEVER, WHATEVER, I PLEASE, AND SO I DID.

SOON, FRIEND COULD NOT TRUST FRIEND, BECAUSE NO ONE KNEW WHO I MIGHT BE...

AND SUSPICION TURNED TO HATRED, AND HATRED TO BATTLE.

THINGS WENT A BIT TOO FAR...

AND THE WHOLE PLACE WENT TO *PIECES.*

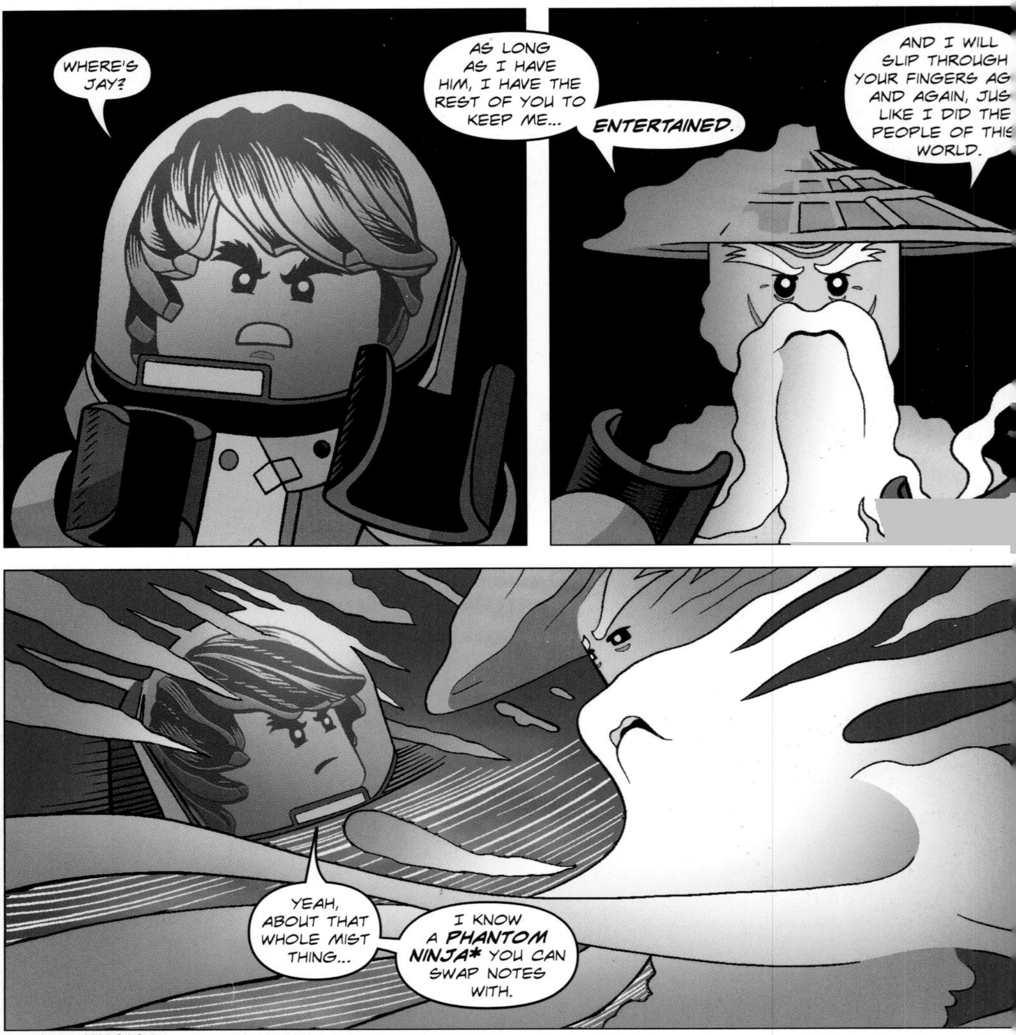
WHERE'S JAY?
AS LONG AS I HAVE HIM, I HAVE THE REST OF YOU TO KEEP ME...
ENTERTAINED.
AND I WILL SLIP THROUGH YOUR FINGERS AG AND AGAIN, JUS LIKE I DID THE PEOPLE OF THIS WORLD.
YEAH, ABOUT THAT WHOLE MIST THING...
I KNOW A PHANTOM NINJA* YOU CAN SWAP NOTES WITH.

*SEE **NINJAGO** #10 "THE PHANTOM NINJA."

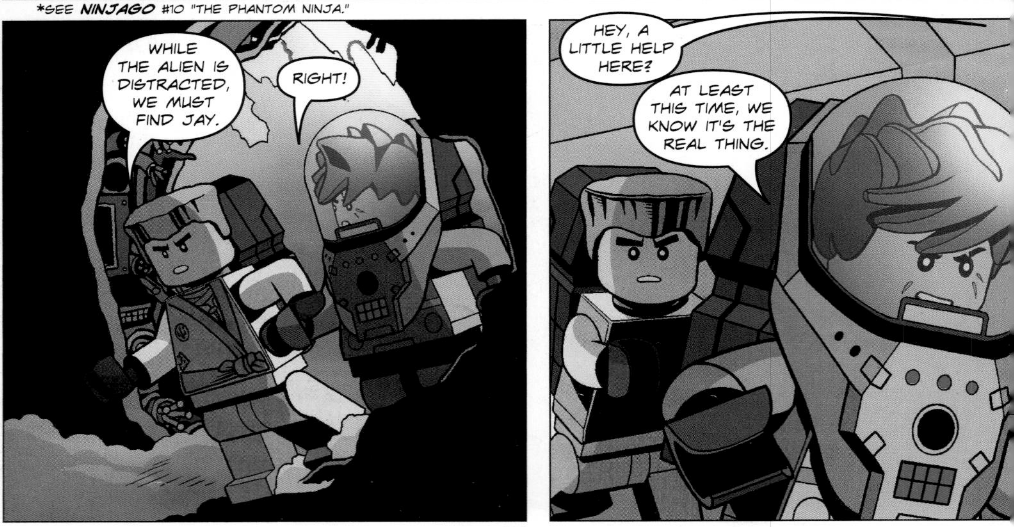
WHILE THE ALIEN IS DISTRACTED, WE MUST FIND JAY.
RIGHT!
HEY, A LITTLE HELP HERE?
AT LEAST THIS TIME, WE KNOW IT'S THE REAL THING.

HEY, PAL, WHY DIDN'T YOU JUST SPIN YOUR WAY OUT OF THIS?

THESE STRAPS ATTACH TO YOUR SKIN LIKE A MAGNET TO METAL.

WOULD HAVE MADE A MESS.

ANYBODY HAVE A PLAN?

THE BEGINNINGS OF ONE.

I HOPE IT'S A GOOD ONE, BECAUSE A TERRIBLE THOUGHT JUST HIT ME...

WHAT IF THAT THING FORGETS ABOUT KEEPING US HERE...

AND DECIDES IT WANTS TO GO BACK TO NINJAGO WITH US?

IT WOULD DO TO OUR WORLD WHAT IT DID TO THE PLANET THIS PIECE OF ROCK ONCE BELONGED TO.

HUH? I THINK I MISSED A CHAPTER.

LATER, JAY-- WE HAVE TO GET BACK BEFORE IT'S TOO--

--LATE. OH, MAN, NOT THIS TRICK AGAIN...
PURELY FOR AMUSEMENT THIS TIME.
I SEE YOU RESCUED YOUR FRIEND, SO I GUESS I WILL HAVE TO FIND SOME OTHER WAY TO KEEP YOU ALL HERE.
LISTEN, WE HAVE MORE IMPORTANT THINGS TO DO THAN PLAY HIDE AND SEEK WITH YOU. WHY DO YOU WANT US HERE SO BAD FOR ANYWAY?
WHY, FOR COMPANY, OF COURSE.
THERE IS NO OTHER INTELLIGENT LIFE HERE. I NEED SOMETHING TO COPY...
SOMETHING TO TOY WITH... OR THE DAYS ARE JUST TOO LONG.
YOU NEED ENTERTAINMEN THEN A WAGE CREATURE...

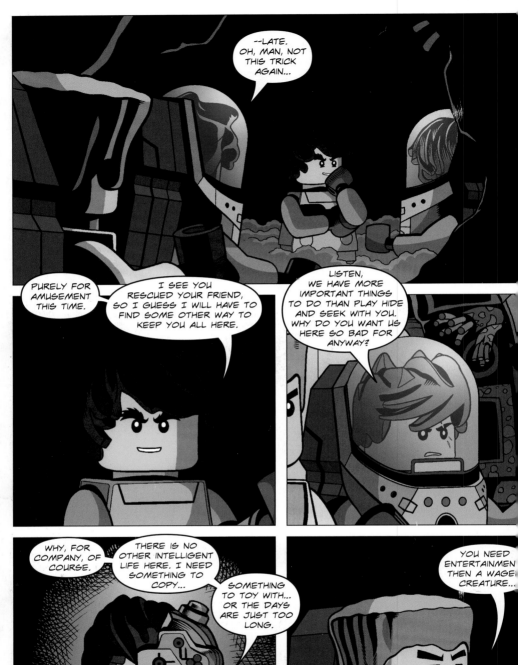

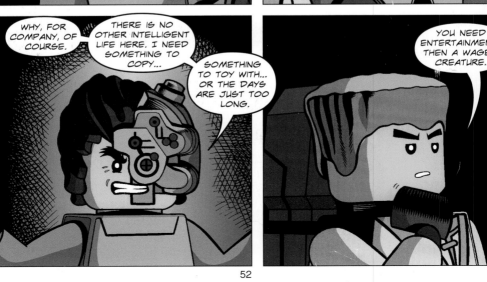

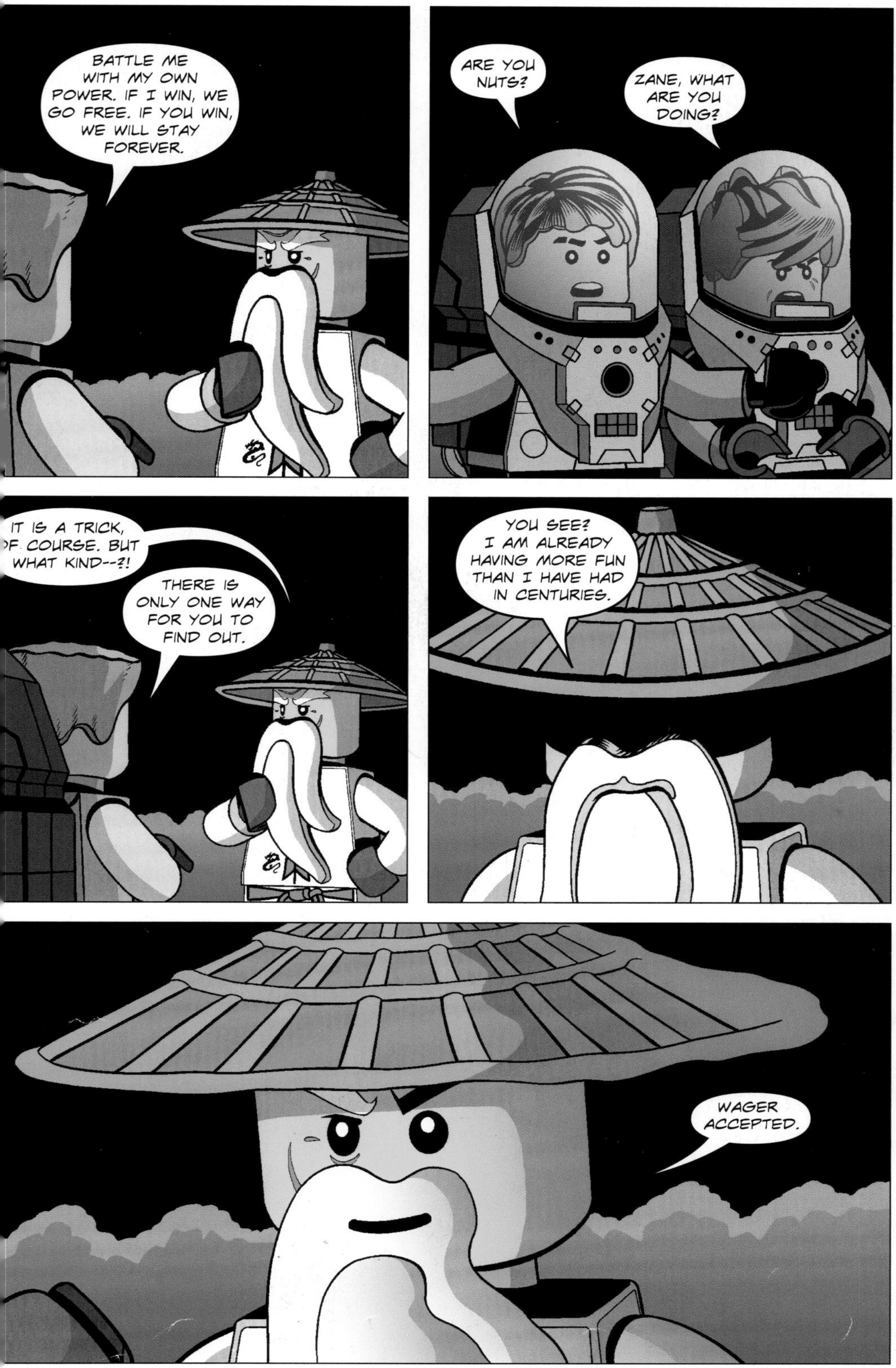
BATTLE ME WITH MY OWN POWER. IF I WIN, WE GO FREE. IF YOU WIN, WE WILL STAY FOREVER.
ARE YOU NUTS?
ZANE, WHAT ARE YOU DOING?
IT IS A TRICK, OF COURSE. BUT WHAT KIND--?!
THERE IS ONLY ONE WAY FOR YOU TO FIND OUT.
YOU SEE? I AM ALREADY HAVING MORE FUN THAN I HAVE HAD IN CENTURIES.
WAGER ACCEPTED.

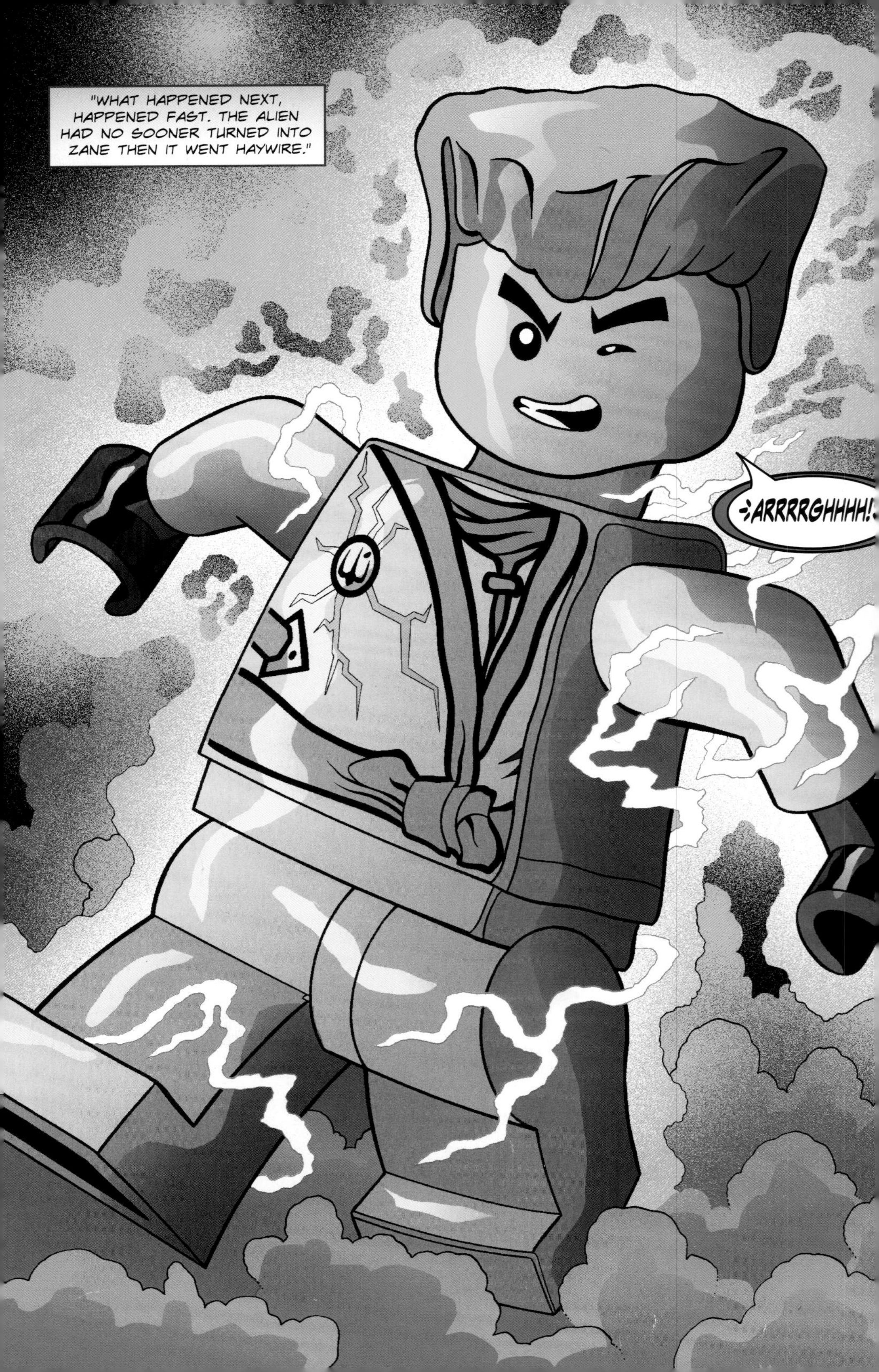
"WHAT HAPPENED NEXT, HAPPENED FAST. THE ALIEN HAD NO SOONER TURNED INTO ZANE THEN IT WENT HAYWIRE."
ARRRRGHHHH!

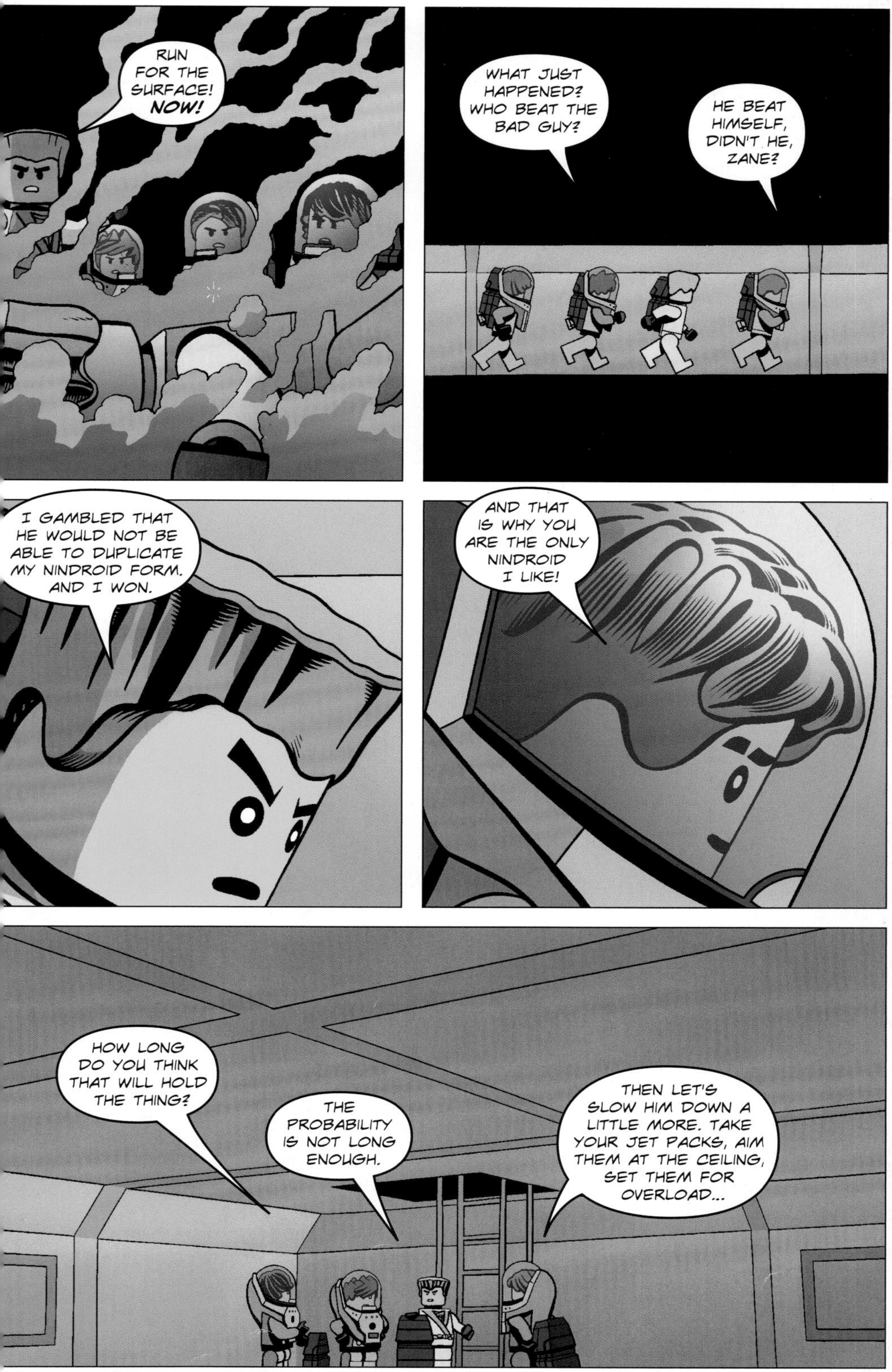
RUN FOR THE SURFACE! NOW!
WHAT JUST HAPPENED? WHO BEAT THE BAD GUY?
HE BEAT HIMSELF, DIDN'T HE, ZANE?
I GAMBLED THAT HE WOULD NOT BE ABLE TO DUPLICATE MY NINDROID FORM. AND I WON.
AND THAT IS WHY YOU ARE THE ONLY NINDROID I LIKE!
HOW LONG DO YOU THINK THAT WILL HOLD THE THING?
THE PROBABILITY IS NOT LONG ENOUGH.
THEN LET'S SLOW HIM DOWN A LITTLE MORE. TAKE YOUR JET PACKS, AIM THEM AT THE CEILING, SET THEM FOR OVERLOAD...

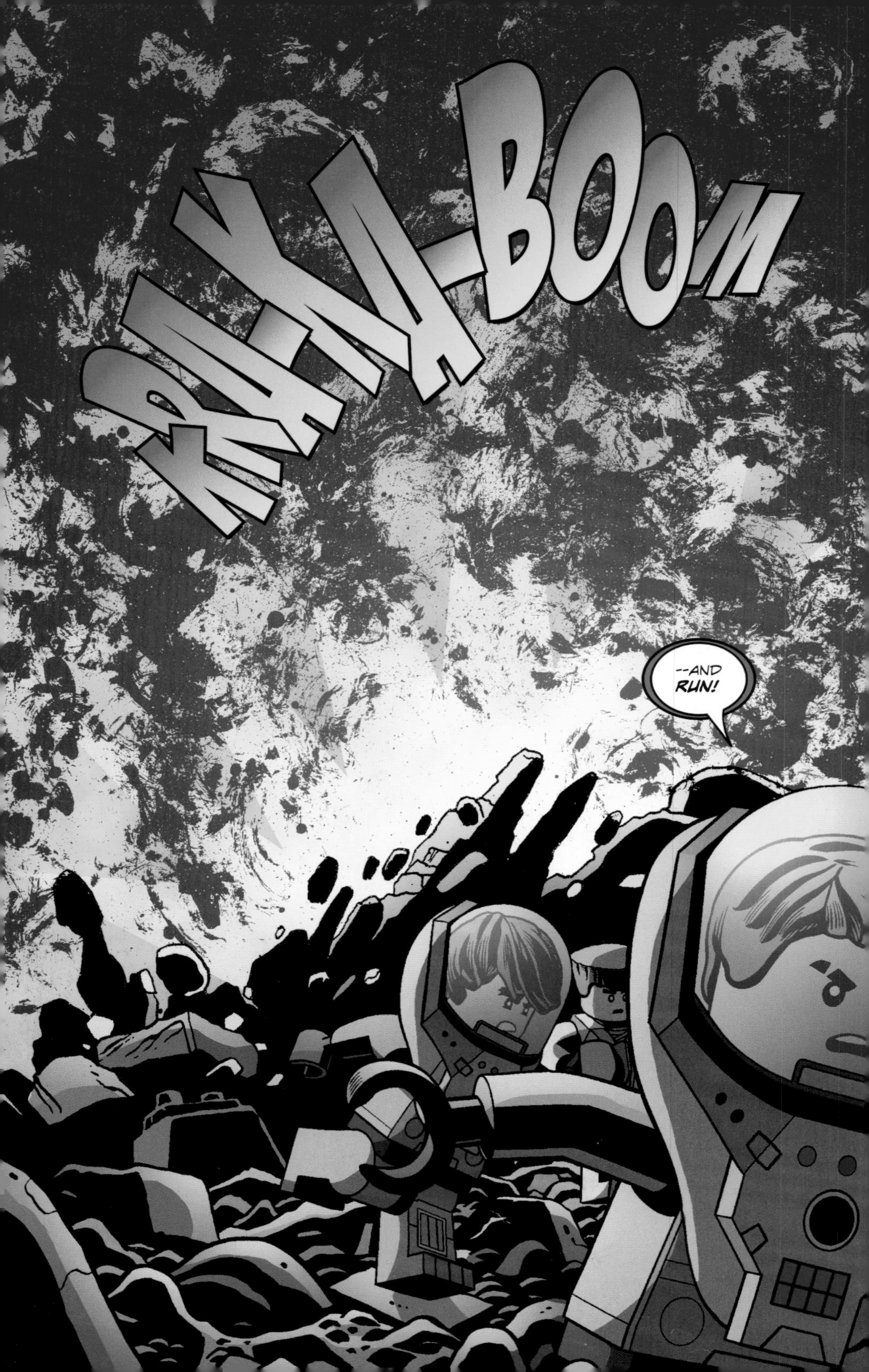
KRAKA-BOOM
--AND RUN!

YOU ~~NK~~--?

NO. THE TUNNEL IS SEALED, BUT HOW DOES THAT STOP A BEING WHO CAN TURN TO SMOKE?

WE HAVE BOUGHT OURSELVES HOURS, MAYBE A DAY.

THEN LET'S MAKE IT COUNT.

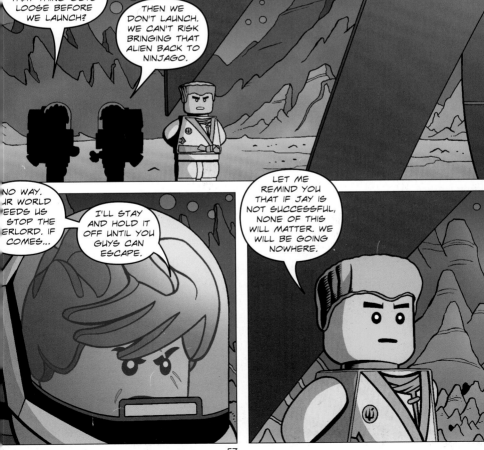

ONE QUESTION, COLE-- WHAT DO WE DO IF THAT THING GETS LOOSE BEFORE WE LAUNCH?

THEN WE DON'T LAUNCH. WE CAN'T RISK BRINGING THAT ALIEN BACK TO NINJAGO.

~~NO~~ WAY. ~~~~R WORLD ~~~~EEDS US ~~~~ STOP THE ~~~~ERLORD. IF ~~~~ COMES...

I'LL STAY AND HOLD IT OFF UNTIL YOU GUYS CAN ESCAPE.

LET ME REMIND YOU THAT IF JAY IS NOT SUCCESSFUL, NONE OF THIS WILL MATTER. WE WILL BE GOING NOWHERE.

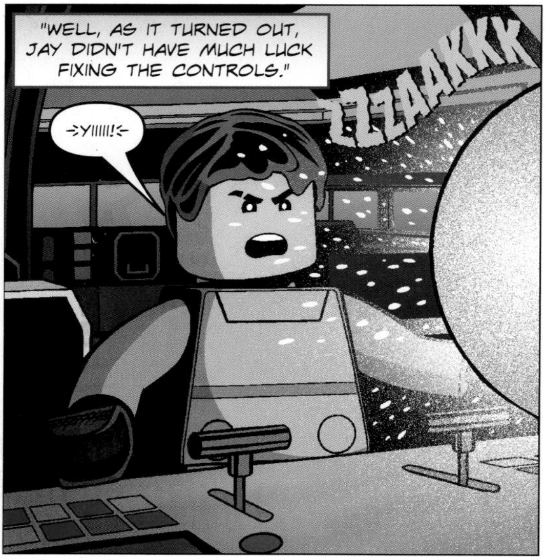
"WELL, AS IT TURNED OUT, JAY DIDN'T HAVE MUCH LUCK FIXING THE CONTROLS."
YIIIII!
ZZZAAKKK

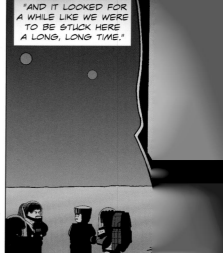

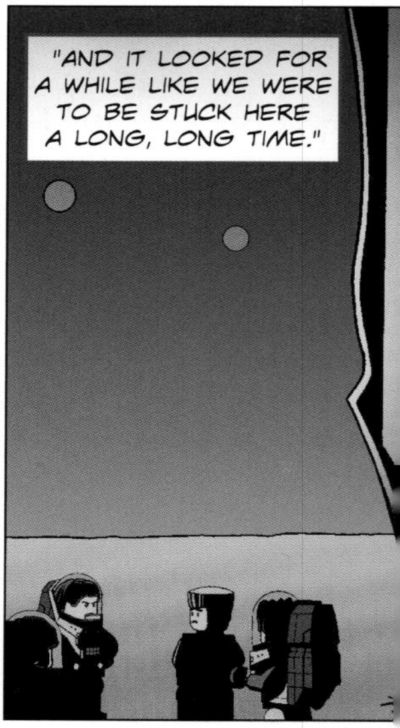
"AND IT LOOKED FOR A WHILE LIKE WE WERE TO BE STUCK HERE A LONG, LONG TIME."

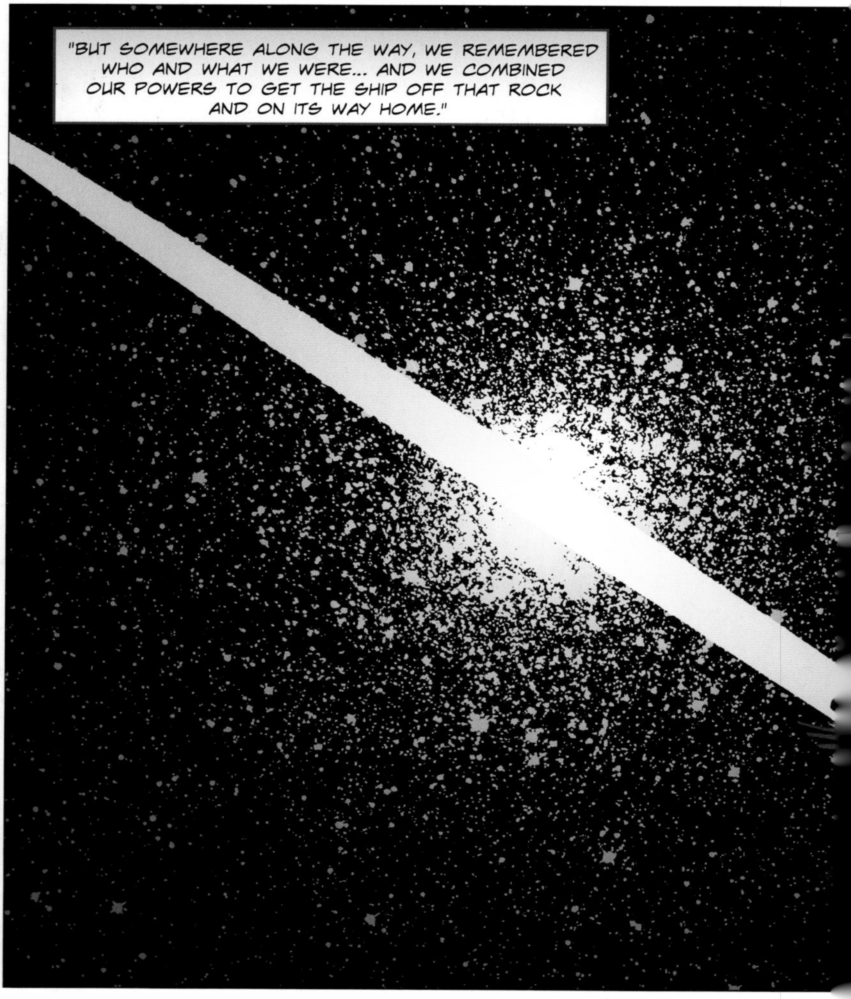
"BUT SOMEWHERE ALONG THE WAY, WE REMEMBERED WHO AND WHAT WE WERE... AND WE COMBINED OUR POWERS TO GET THE SHIP OFF THAT ROCK AND ON ITS WAY HOME."

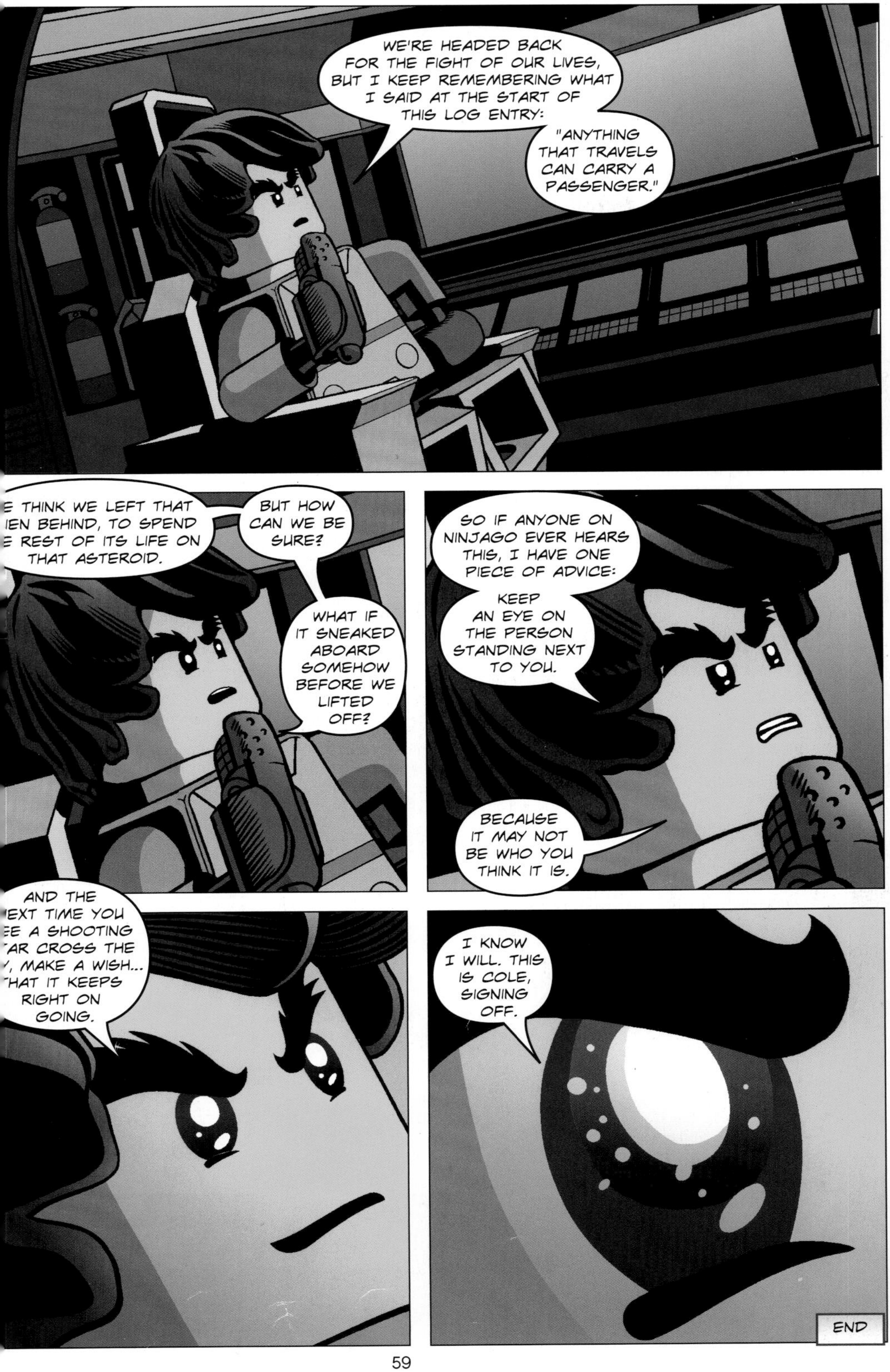
WE'RE HEADED BACK FOR THE FIGHT OF OUR LIVES, BUT I KEEP REMEMBERING WHAT I SAID AT THE START OF THIS LOG ENTRY:
"ANYTHING THAT TRAVELS CAN CARRY A PASSENGER."
E THINK WE LEFT THAT IEN BEHIND, TO SPEND E REST OF ITS LIFE ON THAT ASTEROID.
BUT HOW CAN WE BE SURE?
WHAT IF IT SNEAKED ABOARD SOMEHOW BEFORE WE LIFTED OFF?
SO IF ANYONE ON NINJAGO EVER HEARS THIS, I HAVE ONE PIECE OF ADVICE:
KEEP AN EYE ON THE PERSON STANDING NEXT TO YOU.
BECAUSE IT MAY NOT BE WHO YOU THINK IT IS.
AND THE EXT TIME YOU EE A SHOOTING TAR CROSS THE , MAKE A WISH... HAT IT KEEPS RIGHT ON GOING.
I KNOW I WILL. THIS IS COLE, SIGNING OFF.
END

KIDS GO FREE

with full price adult ticket to LEGOLAND® Parks or LEGOLAND Discovery Cente
Purchase this offer at **LEGOLAND.com/LEGOPapercutzNinjago** now through 12/31/201

LEGOLAND®
DISCOVERY CENTER

Atlanta • Boston • Chicago • Dallas/Fort W
Kansas City • Toronto • Westchester

Indoor Attraction • LEGO Rides • LEGO
MINILAND • 4D Cinema • LEGO Factory
Tour • Play Zone • Birthday Room •
Shop & Cafe

WATCH OUT FOR PAPERCUTZ™

Welcome to the exciting eleventh LEGO® NINJAGO graphic novel by Greg Farshtey and Jolyon Yates, from Papercutz, the ever-hopeful comics company dedicated to publishing great graphic novels for all ages. I'm Jim Salicrup, the Editor-in-Chief, here with the news we've all been waiting for!

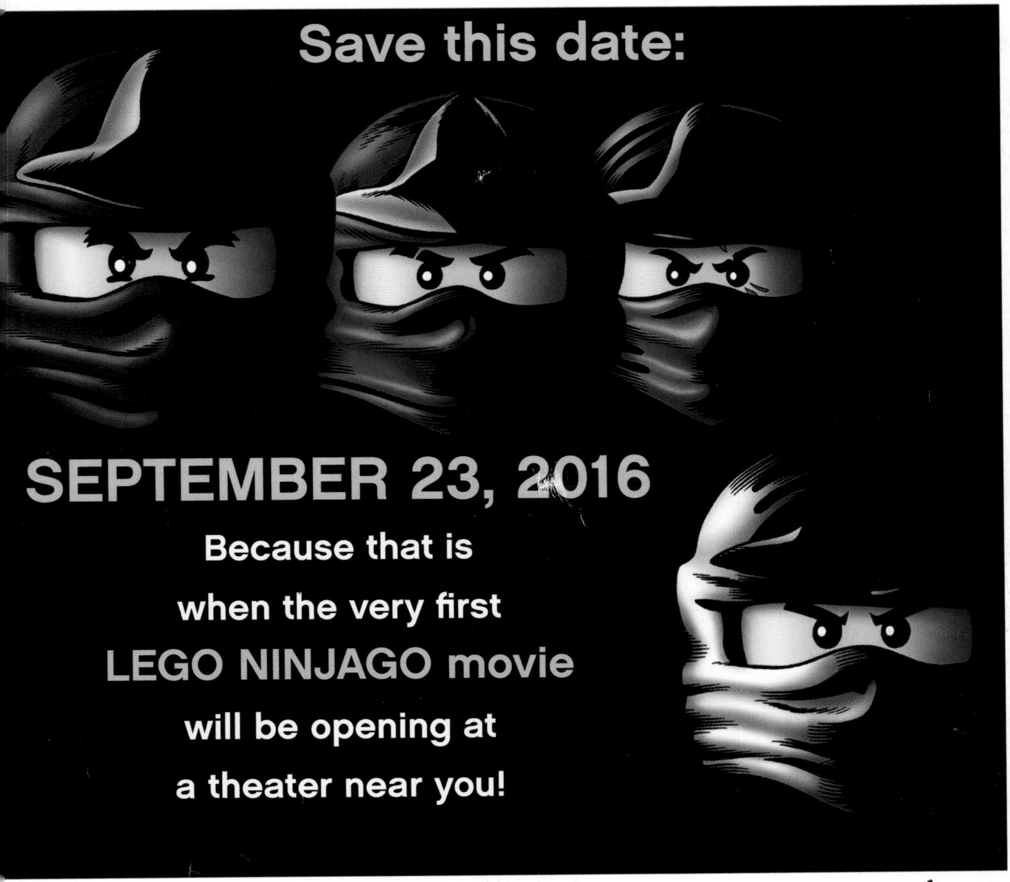

Save this date:
SEPTEMBER 23, 2016
Because that is when the very first LEGO NINJAGO movie will be opening at a theater near you!

Now, that's awesome! Thanks, Jim

STAY IN TOUCH!

EMAIL: salicrup@papercutz.com
WEB: papercutz.com
TWITTER: @papercutzgn
FACEBOOK: PAPERCUTZGRAPHICNOVELS
FAN MAIL: Papercutz, 160 Broadway, Suite 700, East Wing, New York, NY 10038

Know what else is awesome?

LEGO® LEGENDS OF CHIMA!

Check out the preview of LEGO LEGENDS OF CHIMA #2

"The Right Decision" on the next few pages!

Special preview of LEGO LEGEND OF CHIMA #2 “The Right Decisio

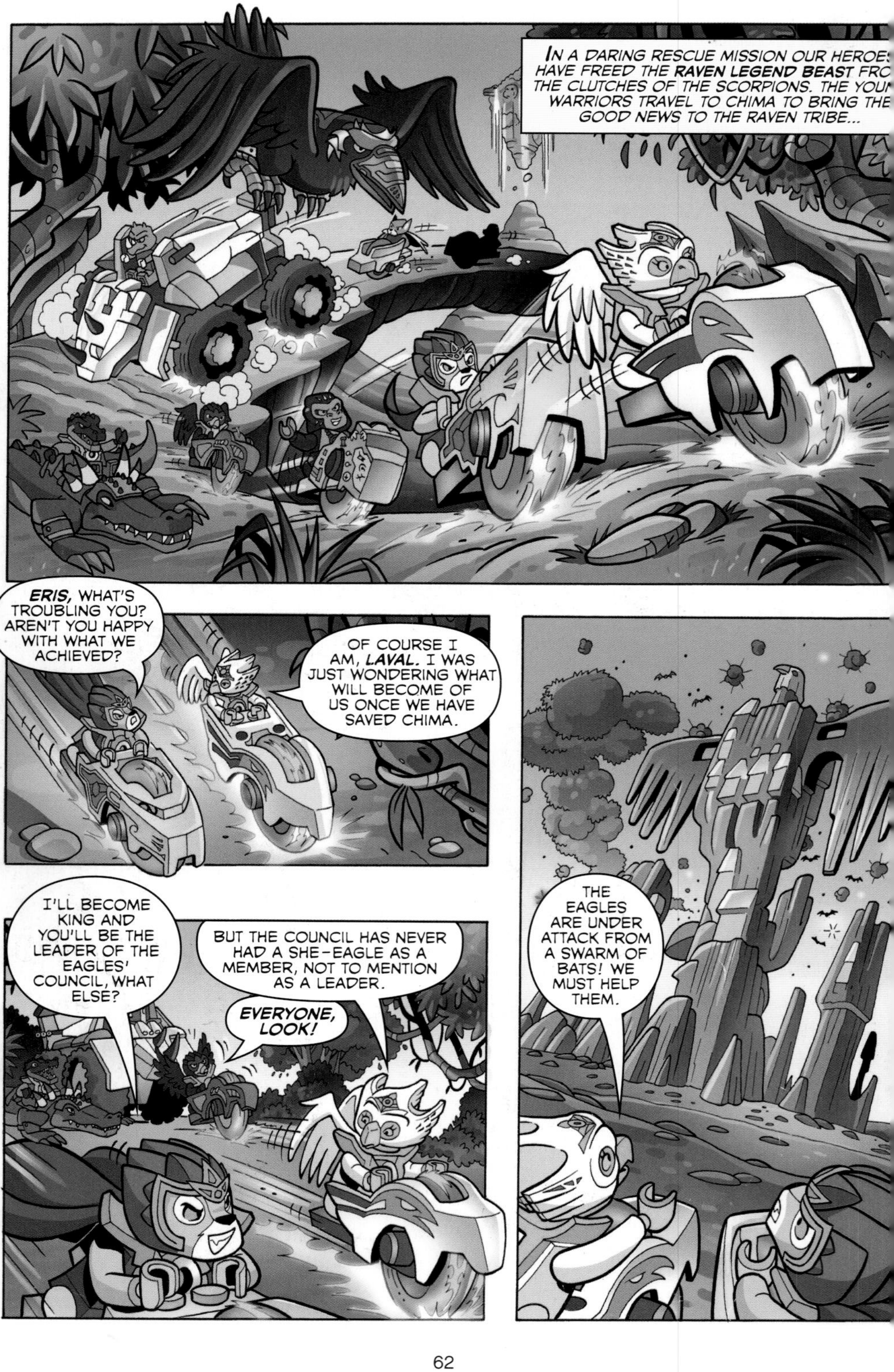
IN A DARING RESCUE MISSION OUR HEROE
HAVE FREED THE RAVEN LEGEND BEAST FRO
THE CLUTCHES OF THE SCORPIONS. THE YOU
WARRIORS TRAVEL TO CHIMA TO BRING THE
GOOD NEWS TO THE RAVEN TRIBE...
ERIS, WHAT'S TROUBLING YOU? AREN'T YOU HAPPY WITH WHAT WE ACHIEVED?
OF COURSE I AM, LAVAL. I WAS JUST WONDERING WHAT WILL BECOME OF US ONCE WE HAVE SAVED CHIMA.
I'LL BECOME KING AND YOU'LL BE THE LEADER OF THE EAGLES' COUNCIL, WHAT ELSE?
BUT THE COUNCIL HAS NEVER HAD A SHE-EAGLE AS A MEMBER, NOT TO MENTION AS A LEADER.
EVERYONE, LOOK!
THE EAGLES ARE UNDER ATTACK FROM A SWARM OF BATS! WE MUST HELP THEM.

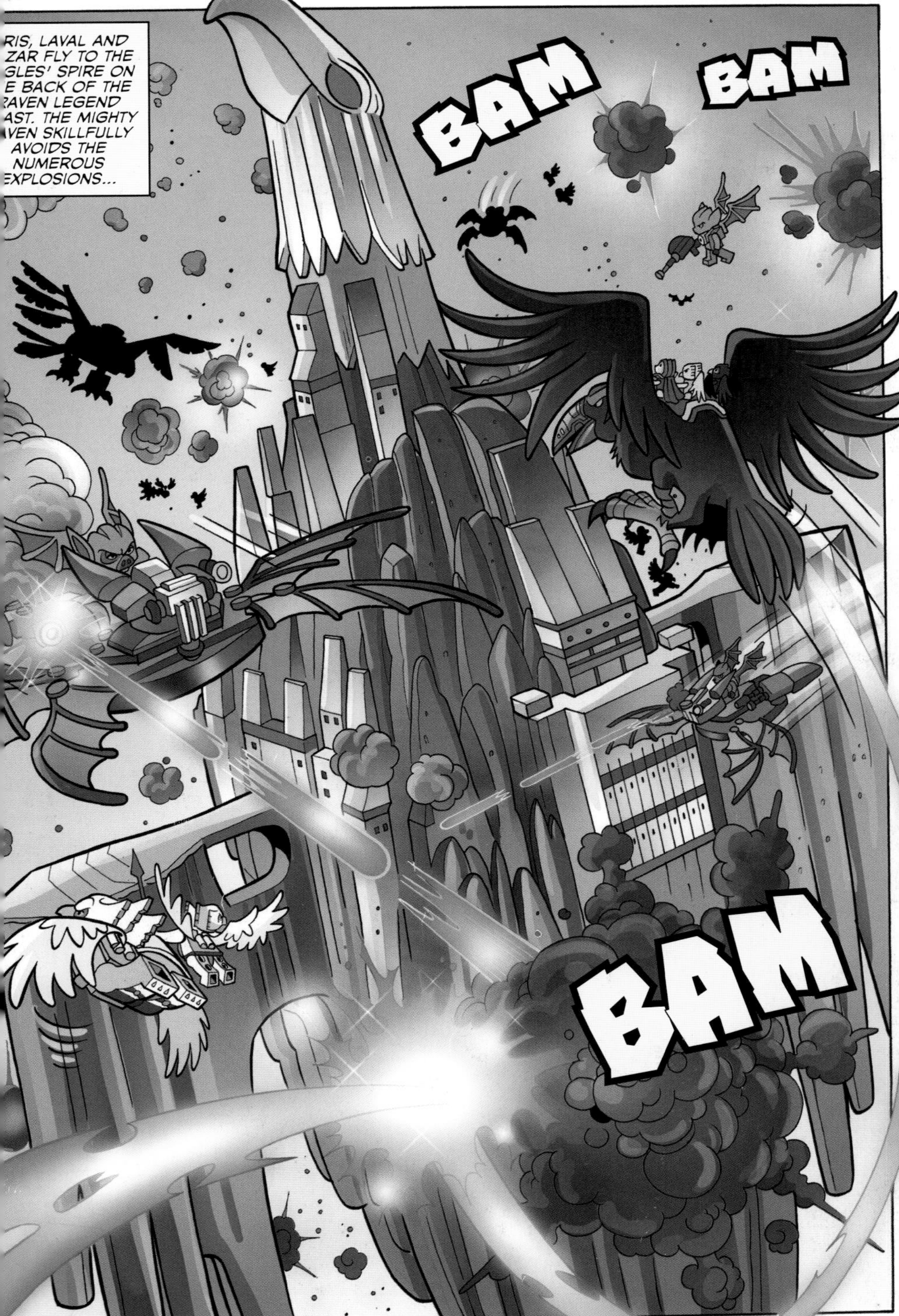
RIS, LAVAL AND
ZAR FLY TO THE
GLES' SPIRE ON
E BACK OF THE
RAVEN LEGEND
AST. THE MIGHTY
VEN SKILLFULLY
AVOIDS THE
NUMEROUS
EXPLOSIONS...
BAM
BAM
BAM

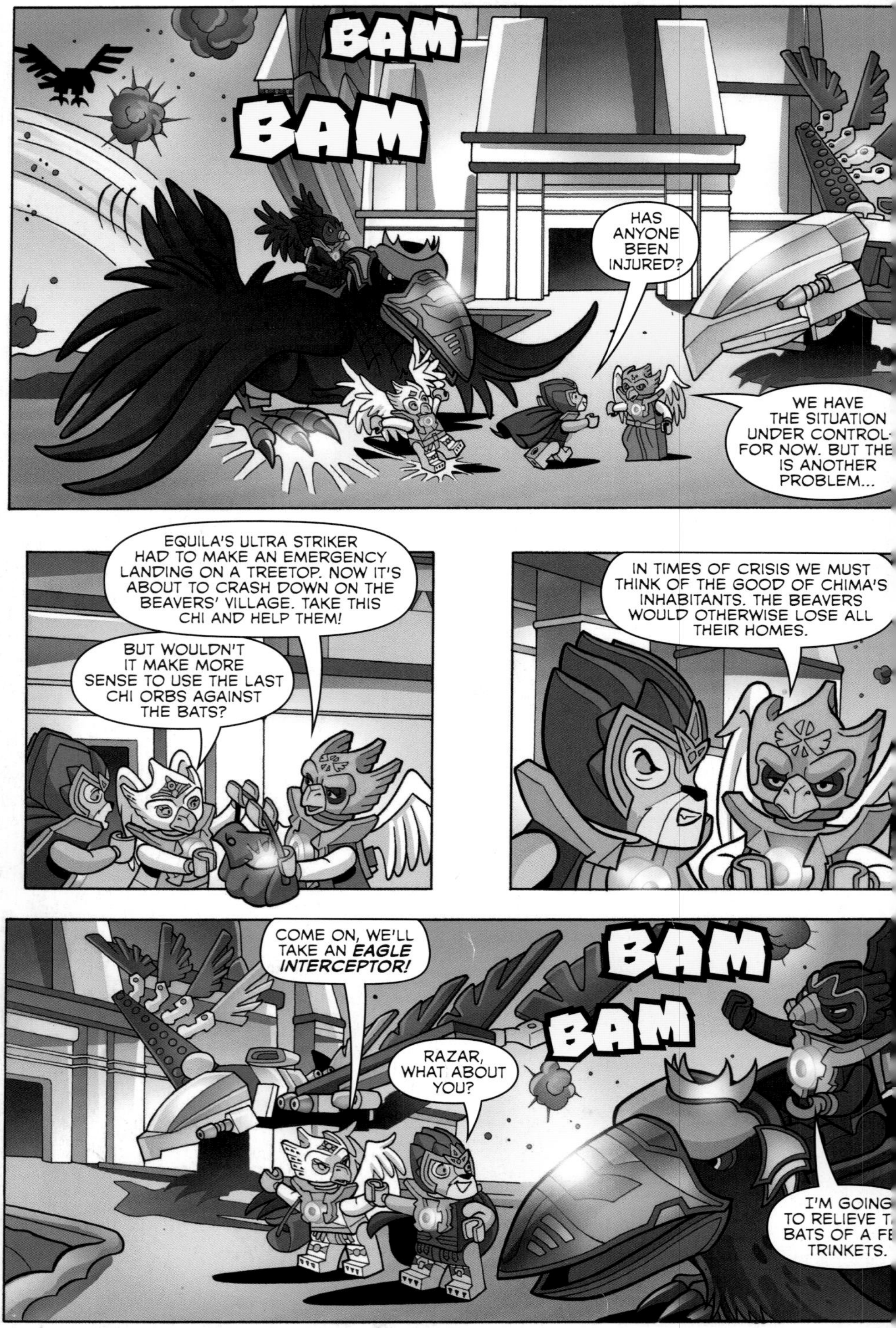
BAM
BAM
HAS ANYONE BEEN INJURED?
WE HAVE THE SITUATION UNDER CONTROL- FOR NOW. BUT THE IS ANOTHER PROBLEM...
EQUILA'S ULTRA STRIKER HAD TO MAKE AN EMERGENCY LANDING ON A TREETOP. NOW IT'S ABOUT TO CRASH DOWN ON THE BEAVERS' VILLAGE. TAKE THIS CHI AND HELP THEM!
BUT WOULDN'T IT MAKE MORE SENSE TO USE THE LAST CHI ORBS AGAINST THE BATS?
IN TIMES OF CRISIS WE MUST THINK OF THE GOOD OF CHIMA'S INHABITANTS. THE BEAVERS WOULD OTHERWISE LOSE ALL THEIR HOMES.
COME ON, WE'LL TAKE AN *EAGLE INTERCEPTOR!*
BAM
BAM
RAZAR, WHAT ABOUT YOU?
I'M GOING TO RELIEVE T BATS OF A F TRINKETS.

Don't miss LEGO LEGENDS OF CHIMA #2 "The Right Decision" available now at booksellers everywhere!

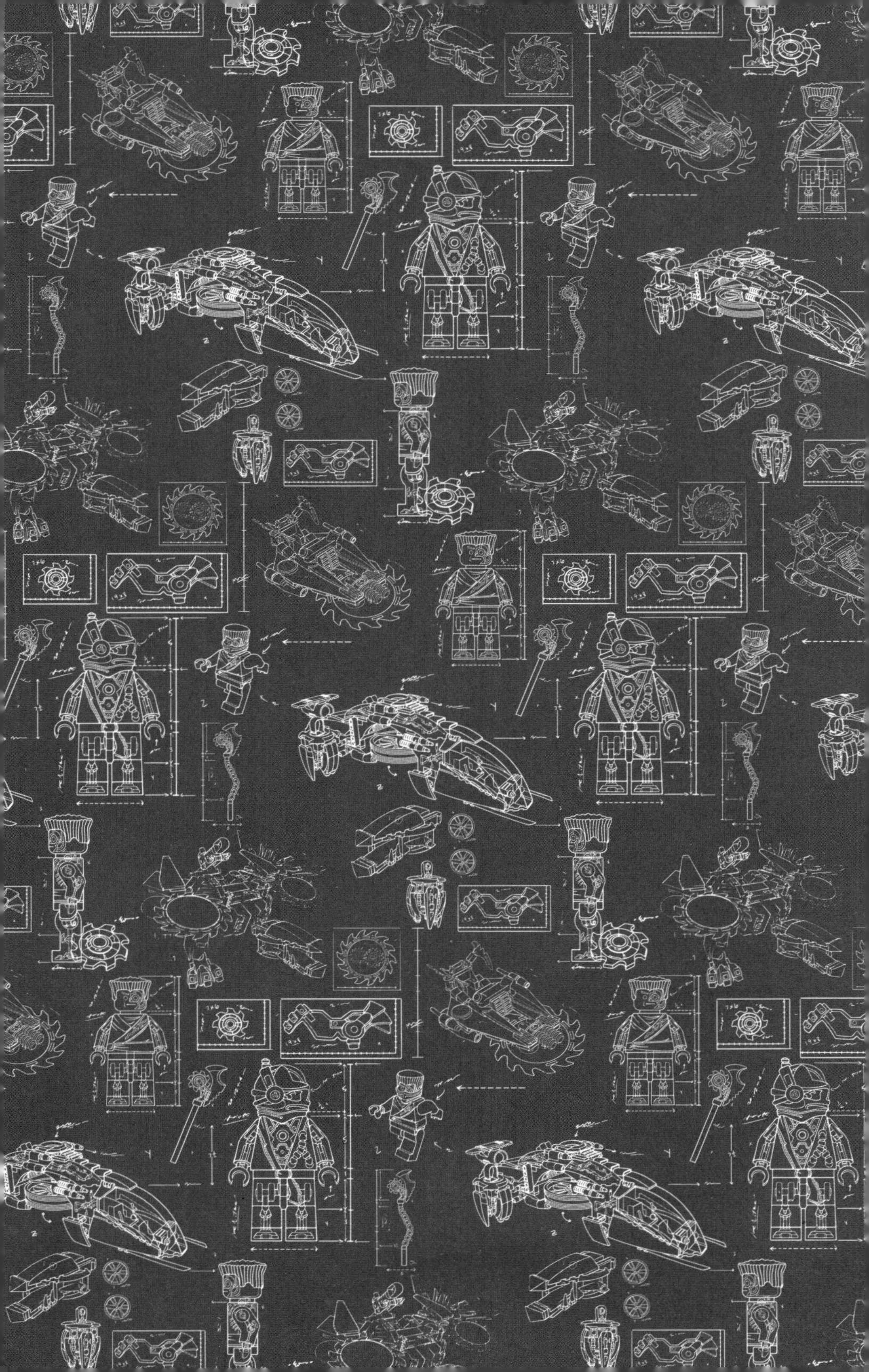

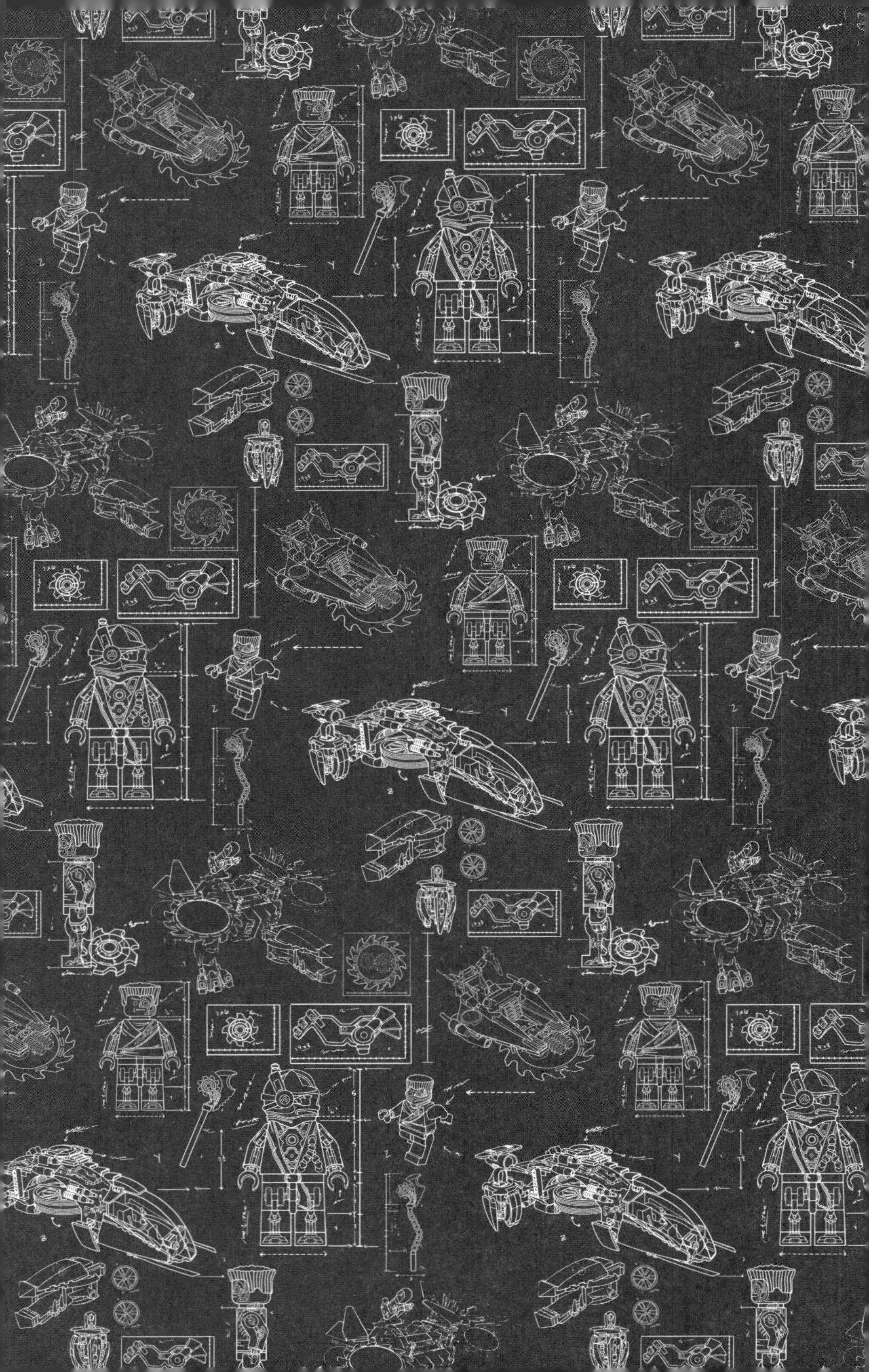